The Glossolalia

The Glossolalia

A Novella

STEPHEN SILKE

RESOURCE *Publications* · Eugene, Oregon

Resource Publications
An Imprint of Wipf and Stock Publishers
199 W. 8th Ave., Suite 3
Eugene, OR 97401

www.wipfandstock.com

PAPERBACK ISBN: 978-1-6667-3121-7
HARDCOVER ISBN: 978-1-6667-2346-5
EBOOK ISBN: 978-1-6667-2347-2

09/30/21

Dedicated to Babu

When are they going to stop making me
mean more than I say?

—Samuel Beckett

I.

I am in my apartment. I look at the apple on the table. It looks right. Things look about right. That perspective is good. This perspective is good. I cast about the room. I try to see myself from all sides. I feel a presence behind me. I sit on the floor, back to the wall, my body activating—the initiation of something present. I take my feet and fall on my face face down. I can smell the smoke and the poison, the fire and the coffee stains on the arcs of my fingers. I am ready. The frame of my back is at an angle, and dynamic for the attack at the bottom and the top. The sense is immense and sweating full, and the back of the end of my mind is a nest of folds. At the end of every word, a death; the end of every line, a tombstone; the end of every act, a confrontation with God.

I arrive at workshop late and can feel their eyes upon me as I enter. It is invigorating. I welcome it. This place should be a dangerous place.

There. Now is everyone on the same page? the Impresario asks.

I approach the stage.

He can feel my fear no doubt. I do not doubt that he has a way in, and I have no way out. I am here to follow. I notice that my hands are still stained. I notice the stillness of the other actors as they watch, how they look at me, how they judge. I am no way forward for them.

I declaim.

Here on this stage I make my soul a chair for the spirit to fill. I declaim a search for salvation, a death march pushing me on, ending each little life I think I know.

I listen. I hearken back, and the back and forth finds me a bit slow. I increase the pace.

And then the response. The responder is too fast. She crests each say too soon. She wears a black hat, and a red blouse, and a red scarf in a knotted necklace. She is inexperienced. Sloe-eyed and waifish, her name is Zozotte. She doesn't recognize my overtures.

I declaim that I have found something. I declaim the certain and the unequivocal. I declaim a hope for life that makes me want to stop and revel in what I am.

The Impresario is holding his head with his hands. It's about that which I struggle saying—the duration of frication, its amplitude.

I remain an empty chair.

He says I play it too heavy. There is no Chekhov. There is no Dostoevsky. There is only you.

What do I have but heaviness?

He reaches his hand out over us. You, you, you—no. You—no. You—yes. No, no, no. Yes. He dismisses eight of us. I remain along with the towheaded brute, Zozotte, Oliver, and Avril. There is a hush of fear and excitement. We are to continue to return. I feel the presence behind me. There is no doubt that further preparation will more fully manifest my impertinence.

On my way home, I stop at a drugstore pharmacy. Under fluorescent tubes, at the counter, I look up and down at the boy helping me. He is heart-wrenchingly ill-composed. He stumbles over each line. His shirt is tight. His hair is shaved but for the poof at the top. He should have a mustache, but instead he wears stubble that does not work in any certain direction.

Can I help?

Will you?

I'll try.

I'm looking for something cheap and easy. Something to give an air of neglect.

At the makeup counter he stumbles to produce the samples that I need. I powder heavily. He looks at me as if he's hoping I buy something.

On the way out, I buy a cheap scarf and wrap it around my chin. I turn around quickly, and he is following me. What else are you looking for? he says.

I do not know.

Home, I put on a velour coat and an ascot. I have tight pants and boots that feel about right.

I throw open the windows over the balcony and though it is cold, it is right.

Heidi was her name, hiding was her game. When Heidi hid, horses halted, hounds and hares hopped hopelessly hither.

I declaim with the mop handle.

I wish to wish to wish the wish you wish to wish, but if you wish the wish the witch wishes, I won't wish the wish you wish to wish.

At the end of every word, a death.

I can feel this in the reptilian fault line of my spine.

I phone Zozotte but she does not answer. Off stage, Zozotte is not talking to me. She has not spoken to me ever since we acted out the scene where I failed to reciprocate her joy. At the tip of the tongue, the teeth and the lips. My cutlery cuts keenly and cleanly. The end of every line, a tombstone.

I am here for you! she had said.

Being here is not anything I am happy with.

I will never let you go, she said.

Letting go of me will give you so much else to focus on.

Her face turned red and she looked at me as if she wanted to slap me. I turned to give her a better angle. Slap, I said.

Yes-yes, I should! she said. If only the slapping would bring us closer together.

No, I said. Slap. Make contact.

There can never be any down time. Every angle, every captured moment is an opportunity to display and live out one's craft. At the end of every act, a confrontation with God.

Never, I say.

Reading and writing are richly rewarding. I eat fresh fried fish free at the fish fry. I buy a box of biscuits, a box of mixed biscuits, and biscuits mixed.

Make the exercises live with the other characters. Have them move the action, the dialogue, the world. It would be something for the world to move with the same pace as the published moments of the work.

I draw the floor-to-ceiling mirror away from the wall toward the middle of my room.

Picasso said something—If a sculpture is well done, if the forms are perfect and the volumes full, if you pour water from a pitcher from above the head, after it's run down, the whole sculpture should be wet.

I wrench my body into an upright pose on one foot and balance. As I look, I focus on the difficulty and then try to forget it. I am blessed with immense control. My breathing acts to keep me on mast, and I withhold myself from falling out of it. I am central to the room. I shift feet, spread arms, and can make myself vertical on either foot. It is magnificent. You know New York. You need New York. You know you need unique New York.

Avril arrives. She wears a low-cut black shirt showing the top of her bra. The shirt has an abstract print of a face below sharp, pointy hair. She tells me to change. I look down. I'm wearing denim overalls, no shirt, house slippers. Where are we going?

Naïve theater is a movement unique to the Internet. In it we have a limitless audience, but we just have nothing really to say. Avril has her arm around me, and we're sitting in a bean bag chair in the corner of a large high-ceilinged loft in the warehouse district adjacent to Chinatown. On her phone we watch the expressions on the faces of various vloggers picture-in-picture as they sell their advertising. Across the room, an artist named Rhony attempts to cast corporate fast food in blocks of petroleum within some piece of large industrial machinery. Oliver drinks beer through a straw while Zozotte assists. Oliver snaps photographs from clever vantage points. Zozotte jumps back and forth from one foot to another. Her black eye makeup is heavy. Ooh, that's good. Ooh, yeah, nice.

The male gaze is offensive, says Avril.

Is she saying this to me about watching Zozotte? Is she saying this to me about what Oliver looks at? Is she saying this to me about what we are watching on her phone? I look over. She is fixated on the phone, so I say Jack the jailbird jacked a jeep. She says do drop in at the Dewdrop Inn, and, I'm getting another drink. I say yeah, one for me too, a little too late, and she's across the room. I put her phone down and look back and down at Rhony's afro. He's pale-skinned, from Ohio. Nordic origins, no doubt. He's wearing some kind of formless silk shirt and fuchsia wristbands. Sometimes I find myself alone even with my friends.

When being narrated to by Internet personalities one wonders why they do what they do. They must endlessly chatter on about the toys they're opening that were given to them by a company in order to generate sales, or they use industry catch phrases to criticize everyone else's art. Their voices are suggestive of flashy vulgarity and conspicuous crudeness. They mix in autobiographical details. They have fun. And there is the artifice of the screen. I would never spend time with these people in reality. I would never spend time with these people. I am not obliged.

I sit watching Avril make two drinks at the open kitchen across the room. At the tip of the tongue, the teeth and the lips. There is no one working any more in the power generator of the soul. It is the predicament that acting faces in this time and place. Where has the salon gone? She hands my drink to Zozotte. Rhony and Zozotte have made a small collection of suspended food sculptures that comment on the artifice of consumerism. They hang from the ceiling. They look like they are frozen in blocks of rusty ice.

Matta writes, *I Shame Myself / I Ascend*. But there are no answers in art, only vague reflections of the impressions of life events. What does Oliver do? With him there is no shame. Oliver documents. Oliver lives on the back end of the action. Even when Oliver acts, there is an intermediary keeping him from the perceiving of real events. He presses his hand forward and there is only the self-conscious specter of his hand—never just the hand—never the full conclusion of the hand demanding to grasp.

He continues to circle the party. Snap snap. Talk talk. I must look closely, he says, but at that same time, not simply notice what I want to notice.

Oliver isn't really here. Oliver is always thinking of the scene where he views the depiction of life events alone in his room, where he finally cracks open the results of what he has captured from life events and then presents them out of context. In this, he cannot ascend. He lives in the vague reflections of the impressions. His products are artful, but they lack immediacy. These images lack a healthy shame.

Zozotte tells Rhony, Now we should add more complexity. Rhony is at a loss. Rhony never thought it could get more complex. His body says so. Oliver edges closer to me. Snap snap. He backs into me. He gestures downward with his camera. It appears that he wants to talk. When one talks to Oliver one listens more and talks less. He turns around to face me and fires off a round of images.

I grasp his camera and push it further downward. I invoke Nietzsche. Read only your life, and from this, understand the hieroglyphs of universal life.

Myself? Oliver asks, holding the camera body with one hand and the lens with another. Help me. Everything points to my fears. But also, there will be a lot of time to wait before my fears become true. All of this will be lost time. I'll get nothing back; I'm losing it for sure. It's been taken away for nothing but for the truth that what I was so sure of was true. This is my fate.

Oliver wrings his hands. He is starting to sweat.

I hear you Oliver, I say. You are the actor for this role. Don't let in the head trip. Own the head.

It's my fate to become very sick, he says. I cry, he says. What I should have been doing with all of my free time before getting sick was to be fully tuned in to the preventative measures that would prevent any chance of illness.

I wag my head. Emphasis on the no.

I gotta workout really hard every day, he says. Maintain a vegetable diet. Meditate, stretch. Work, but not overwork. Sun, but not sunburn. I should play a musical instrument. I should engage in meaning-filled time with my family. Be part of a social network. Get less screen time. Allow little to no sitting. Take naps more often. Wear loose-fitting clothes including footwear that allow my feet to breathe.

Breathe is right, I say, leaning forward and straightening my back.

Yes yes, he says. Full engagement, but lack of stress. Moisturizing. Time spent listening and telling jokes. Heavy laughter. Gargon, I have to figure out what to do. I always dwell on my thinning hair, how I alternate between shallow breathing and heavy breathing. I have unusually oily skin. I have a pale complexion. I struggle to exfoliate my dry skin. I obsess about how there is a numbness and yet simultaneous pain in my stomach. How I have a short life-line, but also wrinkled palms. I have stiff knees and weak knees. My legs have a pronounced vein structure, and I am allover thin skinned. But. He motions back toward the party. I must get the shot.

You must.

I must!

Oliver shrinks back to the party. He will take Rhony aside and try to make art out of shooting him mixing paint in the toilet. I hope it is magnificent.

As I sit, I sit alone. I think about the weight of my body and how I could appear active though reclining in this bean bag chair, back and to the left this way. I shift and alternate my weight so as to make my body sprung. I get up to make a drink, gin and a squelched lemon, then, standing in the middle of the room with everyone surrounding me, I drink it and notice the night is running out of time. It is passing into the day. I see Avril and nod to her. She returns, and I explain how we're running out of time and that the show is tomorrow, and we need to run lines.

Okay, she says, let's run lines. We begin running lines.

We leave the party an hour later and walk down the street toward Avril's apartment. We share Gauloises. I ask her what she thought of Rhony.

Much too much brain, she says, but not too much heart.

That's what it is, I say.

She waves her hands yes. We should not just be extending ourselves for ourselves. We should be extending ourselves for other humans. She tenses. There was a movement in England, she says. It was in the eighties. These women wove yarn threads in a lattice to surround a nuclear missile facility as protest. They enclosed the compound in a communally-created cocoon made of their heart. Craftivism—a group mentality. Now, that was art. I think that kind of thing would be lost on Rhony.

As we enter her apartment, she walks over to greet her dog, Husky.

I remember that I need a shower. I remember that her shower is better than my shower. I enter her shower. Her shower is such that I spend an hour in it. As she sleeps, I take a one-hour shower. In the bathroom I turn the heater on high and say my lines a few different ways. I look thin in the mirror, my hair plastered to the side and the perspiration gaining on my forehead. My nose is too big. It ignores me. My dreams are such that I work tirelessly into the night. My work is such that I dream tirelessly as I work. My night is such that the dream is tireless. Avril is going the way of sleep. Avril sleeps the peaceful sleep of one confident one will not fail. I do not sleep. Lesser leather never weathered wetter weather better.

I find some little pots of makeup. I cover myself in lustrous color. I examine my body. I am thin in my loin cloth; my nose and my mouth are too big for my face. My eyes flash as I roll them from side to side. My Adam's apple strains at my neck. My collar bones are pronounced. In the past year I have been able to diet away any trace of baby fat that might give an air of complacency. My strength is in my hands. My hands have been toned by the gripping and regripping of a series of homemade hand-strengthening machines. I hold a tennis ball and squeeze it twenty-five times in each hand in sets of three. I do a series of thumb-ups. I press palms down on the bathroom counter. In the mirror I drink a tonic in a panicked state. I caress my temples in agitation. I place my hands in a variety of positions, back and around my waist and chest, and then in on themselves. I sit, and make a series of attempts at calmness and then lash out at the mirror. I coil and recoil and then burst out in an angry phalanx.

I turn to my waist. It is a deft pivot-point. Combining the hands and the subtlety of almost imperceptible movements of the waist, I can engender pain, as in the pain caused by nothing being certain in this world. No, no, nothing is certain. At this moment, Avril wakes and after staring at me and processing the gains I have made, makes breakfast and Bloody Marys. I eat the wilted spinach and egg whites, and drink my acidic drink, and we walk to the bus stop on the morning of an altogether implacable day.

I tell Avril I feel nauseous.

That's because you never eat.

Yes, yes, I will apply myself to eat more.

We get on the bus. I feel like there's always someone behind me, I say. Someone oppressive. I feel so mortal. I quote Ellman. It is 5:30 a.m. A loud strong death rattle begins like the turning of a crank. Foam and blood come from my mouth all morning. At ten minutes to two, I die. I had scarcely breathed my last breath when my body exploded with fluids from my ears, nose, mouth, and other orifices. The debris is appalling.

Around the bus, people's eyes circle around and fall on us.

Tell me how you cope in the quiet moments? I ask.

Okay, she says. Let me think of something. Her eyes roll back into her head. Okay, I got it, she says, I go into the bathroom and look at myself in the mirror. I notice that my teeth are crooked.

So, you need braces?

Shut up. She regains composure. She takes measured breaths and continues. I turn the handle on the shower, she says. I'm waiting for the water to heat up. I think that there's no excuse for being fat. Fat is dumb, I think. My eyes fall onto my hands. My hands are beautiful. They are beautiful because I dance. Dancing automatically crafts beautiful gestures. Gesture is the hand equivalent of speech. Good dance is like language lessons. I fall into a rhythm. I like to get into the shower with all of my makeup on, so that the mascara smears down my cheeks in black streaks. It looks incredible. I think about how it really is a window into the soul. These days, a mess of black mascara is not valued for its mysterious virtues. When I scrub the makeup off, my skin glows.

I clap once.

Before the dead time that occurs before every show, everyone works restlessly to knock the final edges off their characterizations, then they shake to shake the jitters out. When time goes dead, I try to drink a sufficient amount of room temp water. Then everything begins to gain momentum. The people who really know how to run the world are busy teaching acting. Such that the Impresario looks at me and asks if I am ready to embody the center.

I am the center, I say.

You are trying to be, he says.

Then what?

He looks up at nothing in particular over my shoulder and quotes J. Peterman. Nothing gets the juices flowing more than throwing a luscious lambswool stole in a moody hellebore print over one's shoulder. Why? Because it is our inside joke. Alfred Jarry, Aphra Behn, Hrotsvitha of Gandersheim, Plautus, which of these ever questioned their role?

I am the laurel wreath on the brow of summer, I reply.

When I find myself on stage, I discover that I know the lines such that I'm lost in the character. I improvise such that nothing stops me. With grace I force myself upon the audience. Others miss their cues, the lighting is poor, a prop disintegrates upon touch. It matters not. I oftentimes take the place of the other actors. I get caught up in an exchange with the Brute. We embrace because he has offended me, and I cannot forgive him. He lacks the eloquence and I lack the ability to shelve my pride and let the offense pass. I don't want to give in, and he does not give up, but our play ends that way.

After the lights go down and we all finish mulling about in praise, I leave and walk awhile. I find myself at a swanky bar. I look at this couple. Hat, tie, heels, leggings, makeup, hair dye, breast augmentation, electrolysis. I wonder what they're dressed up for. Life, I guess, and why not.

I ask if I can buy them drinks.

They look at each other and give a no thank you.

Insist.

They insist not.

I ask, If Stu chews shoes, should Stu choose the shoes he chews?

She laughs an embarrassed laugh. He gives me the what? look. Give us another one, she says.

A big baby buggy with rubber buggy bumpers, I declaim. I'm shameless. I order three champagne cocktails. Give champagne to real friends and real pain to sham friends, I say. I think that's Francis Bacon.

What are you, some kind of clown? he asks.

I notice that I really like being perched upon this stool. I am like a gargoyle. Some kind, I say.

Which circus? she asks.

God's circus, I reply. I have an idea. I want to run an idea by you two.

You've bought yourself the time it takes to drink these drinks, he replies. But I can't let that answer get by without asking what kind of circus that is.

It's the one we're all meant for, I say. You don't sign up and you can't run away and join. You're working towards it from the beginning and it's hard to tell who the intended audience is and why you're performing. And you can do anything you want because you don't know who the ringleader is.

This is life, she says.

Do you two really know why you're doing this? Dressing up? Going out? Drinking to dissipation? Laughing at each other's jokes? Seeing other beautiful people, displaying yourselves for other beautiful people to see? What is it for?

I'm my own ringleader, he says.

Until you're not happy anymore.

I think I've seen you before, he says. I can't tell where from. Do you valet cars?

I want to know if you really know what you're doing? I ask.

He laughs. You're preposterous.

We're out having fun, she says. We had a nice dinner and we'll go home soon.

So, you don't know why.

Why are you asking? he says.

Why don't you know?

They do not drink their drinks. They get up to leave.

If Stu chews shoes, should Stu choose the shoes he chews? These are the people who call human beings consumers. Farewell, I say. Don't hesitate to join the circus if the opportunity presents itself.

I turn back to my drink. I don't feel tired. I feel a presence behind me. I take a sip.

A young guy arrives at the bar next to me and orders a drink. Standing there, he looks at me. He's a still-young silver fox.

I turn away.

He turns to face me. May I sit?

Sit.

Avril told me I'd find you here.

I may be here.

I'm Foster, he says. Foster wears a designer military jacket with audio buds draped around his neck. He's good looking, with happily-messy hair and an artful amount of stubble.

Godot, I say. But I'm sure you know that. I've been waiting here to feel tired enough to go home and sleep.

He takes in the way I look. Wait long enough and it'll be morning.

I look at him back. Are you aware of how you're looking at me?

Foster smirks. I saw your performance tonight, he says. I'm a filmmaker and you fit my film to a T.

Yeah?

It's about a derelict poet—about happiness.

Unfilmable.

But worth trying.

I guess film's seen worse.

Let me tell you about it?

Okay, I say.

He starts. It's about a poet named Insalubre, he says. Yes, he lives on the streets—he's from a rich family but he chooses to be homeless—his poetry wins him an award and he's offered a teaching position which he takes and then regrets every day he shows up to teach—when he does, he inspires the students in his classes to the point that they overthrow the administration of the English Department, but then the students are left with no English Department—the overadministration responds and they are all expelled for their anarchic views—these poets disperse and go on to take guru roles at private universities and various teaching positions in community colleges, or become the heads of poverty-stricken philanthropic organizations throughout the U.S.—they become buried in administrative responsibilities and then end up abandoning their creative work—institutionalized poetry wins—poetry loses—in the world of these poets, writing is forgotten—your character falls in love and is happy.

When do you start shooting? I ask.

I'm in the middle of it right now—but my lead just went to jail—we can't shoot while he's in jail and we're on a tight schedule—and his face has been marred by the sidewalk he kissed while on Benzedrine—he spilled face down out of a stolen car—he has a history of this type of behavior—had—we're on a tight schedule.

And you went to see a play?

It's how I scout—, he says. I ducked in, saw you, and stayed—I milled around a bit and couldn't find you—are you interested?

Some.

He gives me the script and asks if I have representation.

I look down. The film is called *Tone Poem*. The script sure is thick.

There's a lot of white space, he says.

I look up. My agent's called Entrefacado Blathner, I say. He has twenty or so clients. If you can get him to say yes, I'll say yes. Pen? I write down Blathner's mobile number.

I'll make this happen right now, Foster says. Note that we're shooting all day and then all night, so you'll want to be in Los Feliz at nine—and I'll need you until late—in fact, clear your schedule for the foreseeable future.

I'll wait for Blathner, I say. I'm kind of buried in the past— what I've done before.

We'll make all of that go away.

I'll need Blathner's help to get out of what I'm into.

I'm sure there won't be a problem.

Shooting budget?

He laughs in a hollow way.

I leave the bar to walk down Wilshire under an oppressive particulate haze. I consider who I am. I consider who I will be. I consider the character Insalubre. I want to denounce the night for all of its apparent order. As I walk, I see a man pushing a cart. He is a crayon scribble of brown. He positions his hands as if his side is in unconscionable pain. He winces. He walks with a hitch. Tied to his cart is a bag of smarmy recyclables, a scatter of blue and white. I offer him a cigarette. Rubbish, he declaims. He takes one. I thank him. I ask to trade clothes. He tries on my stuff with skepticism. He is disgusted, but I manage to convince him to trade.

It is nine miles to Los Feliz. I make pace. I could take Melrose. I could take Sunset. I head west and walk, and then walk some more, and then turn toward Beverly Boulevard. I begin immediately scanning for something vulnerable. I smell like hell. I purse my lips in a scowl. I feel insufficient to genuinely establish the desperation needed to steal. I begin to fall in step with Insalubre. In spite of his heinousness, he holds his head up high. I make it to Melrose. I can feel the cheap leftovers of LA celluloid and the industrial malaise of early-early morning.

I walk and I walk. I pass La Cienega, I pass Pink's, I pass Paramount. Every word, a death. Left on Wilton, right on Franklin. Wanting won't win. Winning ways are active ways. Every line, a tombstone.

I am rising in elevation. I make it to North Vermont. Every act, a confrontation with God.

I pause.

I wait it out, sitting on an electrical box until a respectable hour.

Then I see Blathner.

We walk into Figaro, the restaurant, and sit down.

He tells me to order something.

I don't have any money.

You can pay me back.

Would I order something if I were really sitting here with you?

He looks at me blankly.

I'll have a water and a salad.

Blathner's eyes bug out as he looks down the prices on the menu. I want a coffee, hot, he says. The waiter waits with pen in hand.

That's all, he says, forcing the menu back into the waiter's hands.

Blathner is not empathetic to the plight of the working professional actor. Blathner wears a cheap pair of slacks and a white polo buttoned at the top, then a threadbare jacket over that. Blathner uses the same flip phone he has used since it became common for agents at his level to use any kind of mobile phone. Blathner appears disinterested, but I know for a fact that the filmmaker Foster has gotten him sufficiently hot for the prospects of this project. Blathner's wisps of black curlies wave in surrender in the air free and then loose when talk gets animated. Blathner should wear a hat.

What are we looking at? I ask.

Seventy-five thousand all told, he says. Twenty-five to start, then the balance when you finish. No royalties unless the film goes over fifteen million gross. I'm taking 40 percent plus office expenses, due to the inconvenience of Foster Green. He demanded a script reading at 2:30 a.m. And then there's your inability to keep a bank account in the black. Managing your allowance, paying your bills, all the stuff you'll need me to do now that you've actually found profitable work. And the script is shit, he says. No commercial value. It's barren of catch phrases. There's no clever banter. If it weren't for the money, I would never approve. What you need is a clever caper with a strong character and first-person voiceover narration. A sure-fire money maker is when the narrator gets the best of the cops. On film, the cops should always be the bad guys. Your characters should always one-up the authority figures. And every leading lady should be a hot number. Films should be easy on the eyes.

Blathner develops those little berms of viscous spit at the corners of his mouth as he speaks. He talks unchecked. Why're you wasting your time with this arthouse shit? You're not at this point in your career Gargon. Sure, you pulled off this deal, but you're gonna spend all this money on snow cones and sparklers before production is even finished. You need to do commercials. Stuff they'll run over and over again. Land a TV show so you have a platform.

The berms of viscous spit continue talking even when he's drinking his coffee. Blathner wants to come with me to the set. I say I'll meet him there. He tells me where to walk. He says he'll get my retinue. He wants me to do something about how I smell. I take up a napkin. He allows me to gingerly hold the back of his bloated head with one hand and then lovingly wipe the corners of his mouth with my napkin. It is a quiet, intimate moment. I am profoundly touched by his docility. He is at a loss for words, so he keeps talking. He seems astonished by my gentle touch and by my concern. We part ways in an armistice. I trust he will do the right thing.

I leave and walk up the street, then sit down on the curb. Insalubre hides his inner wisdom from me. I wrestle him to interrogate him more. Fred fed Ted bread and Ted fed Fred bread. Near an ear, a nearer ear, a nearly eerie ear. He will not open up, so I open up unto him as a flower. He, the bee. I must give him a strong presence. I make certain that I can get into a conniption fit at the drop of a hat. I beg and I scream and Insalubre begins to reveal himself. I walk around Los Feliz for a while.

I arrive on set. Well-appointed film sets are artistic desolations. They offer up no apples. The only aesthetic food is the surveillance, the continual filming and the audio collecting and the filming of the filming. These are the days of the ultimate acting challenge in my estimation. The gestures I make and the noises and the sounds and the miscues that I offer up are the life of the upper register of play.

Oliver arrives in a bad mood. He has taken my place in the play. Zozotte and Avril make friends with the production staff. They plan on trying on most of the clothing in the production's quiver in order to steal that which makes them happy. Blathner is demanding a rewrite. Does the script matter? I question.

I grab the Brute and walk him off to the side. I run possible lines with the Brute. The Brute is magnificent. He has a square jaw and little hateful eyes, and he fiercely opposes me. I provoke the Brute. He stutters. I feed on him. There are grunts and yelling, guttural utterances. Insalubre grows in depth and candor the more he has to reach out. I see Susie sitting in a shoeshine shop. In fact, Susie works in a shoeshine shop. Where she shines, she sits, and where she sits, she shines.

We sit in a dirt patch in the garden. Without saying it, the Brute challenges me to provoke him.

I provoke; You are rowing a boat upstream. The river flows at three miles per hour; your speed against the current is four and one-quarter. You lose your hat on the water. Forty-five minutes later you realize it is missing. Execute the instantaneous, acceleration-free about-face that such puzzles depend upon. How long does it take to row back to your floating hat?

The Brute stammers. He jams his fists into each other. With his mechanical chops he gestures with a pencil and paper. Simple, he says.

How so?

The algebra is routine.

No, do it in your head. But if you mentally start calculating the numbers and the fractions, you are lost. This is a problem about reference frames. The river's motion is irrelevant—as irrelevant as the earth's motion through the solar system or the solar system's motion through the galaxy. In fact, all such velocities are mere foliage. Ignore them, place your point of reference at the floating hat—think of yourself floating like the hat, the water motionless about you, the banks an irrelevant blur—now watch the boat, and you see at once, that it will return in the same forty-five minutes it spent rowing away. The goal is a mental flash, achieved somewhere below consciousness. In these ideal instants one does not strain toward the answer so much as relax toward it.

The Brute is stone. He looks at me with an expression of hurt. You need to be more charitable in your exchanges, he counters. I sympathize, but I had to establish the authority inherent for the role. Insalubre is not charitable. Insalubre is a wrecking ball.

He hits me in the face. I fall out of lotus position and onto my back. He jumps on top of me. I relish how the Brute has taken offense. He twists my arm up over my face and I feed on this. I begin to breathe hard as he manhandles me. What about this kind of math? he asks. Crew gather around as the action intensifies. I wrestle myself to my feet so as to gain an advantage. I am able to lean on the Brute, to the point where he falls over still holding onto me, and we destroy a potted plant. The adrenaline has flooded my body to the point where it feels I could lift the Brute up into the air and crush him with my elbow. I am able to wrest myself free and I come at him fast, but a prop boy catches me and then some other crew members surround us to keep us separated. Avril is clapping. The Brute's face is red, and he is not joking anymore. I am not able to fight against the three crew members who are holding me back. Foster appears. What's going on guys?

The shoot is taking place at a McVilla off a winding hillside street. Peach stucco, queen palms, tile roof. The craftsman bungalow next door has also been secured for dressing rooms. In the break before a meeting my eyes glance down at the legal and contractual rider Blathner's assistant has written.

```
Purchaser is to provide the following items
daily for Godot Gargon's dressing room (with
access for entourage) at no cost to Artist:
Thirty-four (34) bottles of room temperature
bottled water (not Crystal Geyser). Full-
service espresso machine w/ porcelain serv-
ing cups (no sugar). No less than three (3)
honey bears (organic) at all times. One (1)
pint of organic whole milk (Ice down organic
whole milk in a large plastic bus tray or
ice chest.). One (1) bottle of echinacea
capsules. One (1) fruit platter of NOTE:
uncut raspberries, blueberries, ripe avoca-
does, papayas, mixed variety of pears (all
must be organic). Three (3) medium, organic
beets. A quarter (1/4) pound ginger root.
Six (6) large, white bath towels. Six (6)
face towels. Six (6) hand towels. Three (3)
bars oatmeal soap. One (1) slow cooker pot
of homemade vegetable soup (tomato-based) w/
beef, chicken, or ham w/LOTS of broth. One
(1) slow cooker pot of homemade cream of to-
mato soup. Six (6) sets of vintage porcelain
or stone bowls & spoons (no plastic). Six
```

to eight (6-8) empty to-go boxes (in a bigger box placed under table). Six (6) plain
organic yogurt tubs (not Greek. Ice down all
yogurt tubs in a large plastic bus tray or
ice chest). One (1) juicer. vintage cutlery
& serving plates, including paring knives
for cutting up fruit & vegetables. A mixed
variety of vintage costume hats size 6 ¾ inch
(masculine or feminine, flamboyant, homely).
One (1) ironing board with iron & electrical outlets & one (1) spray bottle w/ dis-
tilled water. One (1) chaise longue. One (1)
six-foot sofa. Four (4) easy chairs w/ arm
rests. One (1) coffee table. One (1) large
arrangement of colored flowers (no chrysan-
themums, carnations, or sunflowers). One (1)
hot water kettle. Full organic salad service
for six (6) including all of the following
leafy vegetables: baby spinach, mesclun,
rocket, alfalfa sprouts, butter lettuce, red
leaf, endive, escarole, cilantro, romaine.
A variety of onions & herbs in season. One
(1) bottle premium olive oil (imported, not
Spanish). One (1) bottle premium balsamic
vinegar (NO OTHER DIPS OR DRESSINGS). Four
(4) bottles of chilled vintage Poilly Fuissé
(1963-1986; no 1973). No fluorescent lighting. Two (2) rounds of black electrical tape.
Two (2) packages of unscented baby wipes
(premium, organic). Tall leafy plants as
décor. Two-dozen (24) unshucked oysters on
ice. One (1) oyster shucker (the tool). Frozen strawberry margarita machine. Room must
be draped in black or white floor-to-ceiling
drapes. Barbells & dumbbells w/ a variety
of free weights & a weight bench w/ incline
& decline bench press setup in addition to
leg workout functions (Home gym machine w/
these functions OK). Freeze-dried strawber-
ries. One (1) variety box of Pop Rocks. One
(1) pack each of chocolate, natural, & mango

bidi cigarettes. Three (3) one-liter bottles
of club soda in glass bottles (Ice down club
soda in large plastic bus tray or ice chest).
Twelve (12) cleaned & dressed radishes. Ten
(10) AC outlets. One (1) large technology
grade bottle of rubbing alcohol. One (1)
box of shop towels. One (1) box of cotton
swabs. One (1) box of Q-Tips. One (1) large
stretchy, collagen protein bandage (must be
twelve (12) feet or longer). One (1) box of
plastic drinking straws. One (1) bucket of
12-piece hot fried chicken (dark meat only).
This agreement cannot be amended, supple-
mented, or varied except by an instrument in
writing signed by Entre Blat Entertainment,
Inc.

We meet to talk in Foster's trailer, which has been rigged up with a bevy of digital recording equipment. It is Insalubre, Lucia, Foster, and a quick-moving youngster with a bandana tied over his head and a big belt full of wires and tape. Insalubre wears tight flannel shorts with no belt, leather strappy sandals, a buttoned-up oxford, and a sweater vest. The room is warm from flooded light, and there are harsh shadows. Lucia is dressed comfortably in an oversized sweater, no bra, ripped denim shorts, and battered boots. Foster wears a corduroy suit with a fuzzy dangling scarf and audio earmuffs.

Lucia takes me in.

Bum hair or film hair? I ask.

She is unsure, then she decides. The kind of hair that makes the audience question their own choice of hair.

Did you get that? Foster asks the youngster. We need a softie and a backlight to make this pop a bit. The youngster nods while strapping a big expensive thing to some legs. Moving on, Foster says.

I can feel Foster's insecurity. He starts in. I want you to fill in the gaps that still exist in the character.

I meet eyes with Lucia and two flashes go off. She seems to want to find me reprehensible, but I can see that she does not. In fact, I say, no one will be able to do what we will do.

We begin about Lucia's struggle to keep herself from giving herself away to anything.

She saves herself for herself, Foster says, and the youngster presses a button with his thumb. Something over on the other side of the room snaps.

She nods.

I nod.

Lucia is Insalubre's lifelong foil. Neither can move without supplanting the other.

We all move our feet so the youngster can run a cord taped to the floor under the table we're sitting around.

I gotta be in you and Lucia at the same time, Foster says. For us to be one, we gotta all inhabit a single space.

I ask about Lucia's past lovers.

She narrates how she has abandoned them and every family member who ever wanted anything like a meaningful relationship. It cuts her, and she hurts whenever she thinks about it.

Say that again, Foster says.

She gathers herself. My lovers have never left me, she says, and my family is always kind. It's always been *me*. I suffocate myself.

Lucia is a profound dreamer. She has never made herself available beyond brief moments in time. Insalubre cares. He wants her to get out of herself. But his ambitions and his headstrong nature force her to question just how much he cares. He insists she has a child somewhere. She insists he is a child. She insists.

Ask what hurts you the most, Foster says to Lucia.

Lucia crosses her legs at the knee, then uncrosses them. She shifts her fingers over her face and chin to hide her mouth. Who has hurt you most?

Insalubre nods. Insalubre's brow quivers. My brother.

China ball's in place, the youngster says.

A 360-degree dome camera with a swivel head drops down from the ceiling between us all. The servos spin to focus the lens.

Foster ignores it. Tell me about him.

Insalubre declaims. The problem I always face is the problem of my brother. My brother is the alternate version of myself. He is what I could have been. He is what I'm not and yet we are so similar. My brother is the one I strain not to duplicate, but the one whom I should most fiercely love. He is that person, whom, because of my human failings, I must keep at a distance. It is because of my brother that I aim to be plurilingual. I am always desiring distance and yet always needing in some capacity—a never ending buoy on insecure waters. The written word seduces as my way to get away from him. Getting away from him is my élan, my exteriority, my embodied memory—my work as a poet. The challenge is to learn how to act like a child. It is the key to art and the key to poetry. It is everything that can be summed up in one simple phrase, one jot of punctuation, one line break.

What is the vehicle that moves this portion of the narrative forward? I ask.

Foster recoils like he broke trance, Insalubre's rich father has joined with Lucia in an effort to give Insalubre money to support himself—Insalubre won't take it—the father is humiliated when, for his birthday, Insalubre gives the father flowers he has poached from the roadside—Insalubre insists that rejecting this gift demonstrates a paucity of soul—Lucia wants peace but also wants the money.

Why? I ask.

Lucia breaks in, Because she wants a country house. She wants an apartment in the city. She wants monogamy. Insalubre doesn't want this?

No, Foster says, he doesn't want this. Insalubre hates everything this stands for.

Why? I ask.

Lucia tightens up. A good actor is a child. No self-consciousness. Because good watchable people are children. A good audience wants to watch children at play. What they're looking for in a good film is to watch good children going up against bad life.

When we work together, we should be like bicycles mangled together on a plinth. Inextricable. Tragic. A spectacle.

This is a workable direction, Foster says. The youngster gives a thumbs up. Here's your revisions, Foster says. He pushes paper toward me. I recoil.

Right, he says, Blathner told me about this. Foster motions to the youngster. Give a copy to Avril and a copy to Brutus. He turns to me. Happy?

As we exit the trailer, I attach myself to Lucia's arm. I say, James just jostled Jean gently. And I tell her we need relationship therapy.

She laughs and throws her head back. Already?

No joke, I say. There's this group in Saskatchewan that helps couples get past dependence on the trappings of superficiality. They practice Privation Therapy—P.T. We need to go if we're to make any progress.

Now?

Now.

The shoot is already behind schedule.

Do you want a failed film on time or a fine film on failed time?

You're mad. No. You know what? I want a fucking fine film on time. That's the least we can do.

Listen to me, I say, this is a very important thing.

Listening.

Heartfelt ineptitude has its appeal and so does heartfelt skill. But what you want is passionate virtuosity. John Barth.

Lucia balks. This is not my decision.

I take responsibility.

Fear is my weakness, she says. It drives me.

Get over that shit. It will only get you so far. The shit must be controlled. Like how a jazz musician holds a toilet plunger over the end of his horn. The plunger deflects the shit, but it also draws it out.

If Foster says so, I'll do it.

It doesn't matter, I say.

Foster's the boss, she says.

I throw my hands into the air. Acting, I say, is not secret information. It is confidence. I shall, rather than I cannot. I will press on beyond what I know. I will go on after my instruction, and perhaps overcome it. Yes, I will overcome the limits of my training. I will fight my way until I am free. Even if it means I free myself from the director.

Of course, but.

How can a clam cram in a clean cream can?

A clam can cram in a clean cream can if it can. If it can't it crams in a cleaner, clearer cream can than that can if it can.

We break away and it appears that the youngster has captured all of this. He's holding his camera at his side wiping sweat from his face. Screen test is in the can, he says, so to speak.

Roll eyes.

I get back to the dressing room and Zozotte and Avril and Avril's Husky are lounging around juicing. If you're poor, you're called crazy, Avril says. If you're rich, you're eccentric.

Zozotte flicks her nose. As my father would say, the nail that sticks out gets hammered in.

I tell Avril about P.T.—that the three of us need therapy.

Me, you, and Zozotte?

Me, you, and Lucia.

Who's Lucia? Oh, right, we were just practicing her. No, she says. Wait. Let me ask Husky. Nope. Husky says no.

Get out, I say.

They laugh.

I turn to leave and then I walk around outside to try and find Blathner. I decide to change. I walk down the hall and a PA trails me and I step foot onto the patio. Oliver is filming the Brute. The Brute is reading Insalubre's lines.

The nail that sticks out gets hammered in, says the Brute.

That line already feels stale.

I say hello, and keep walking toward wardrobe. Oliver turns the camera toward me as I walk away. I do not acknowledge it.

Wardrobe is in the pool house and I realize that the water would feel fabulous on my skin, in the sun, in the hotness of the day. I can't remember the last time I stretched.

PA, I say.

The PA materializes. She grips her tablet in the crook of her arm. She wears a beret and an oversized weathered T-shirt with the sleeves rolled up. Under that, pegged highwater slacks and purple eight-eyelet Doc Martens.

Look at me, I say, I have nothing to wear. I tell her to find something comfortable and relevant.

Got it, she says.

Also, I say, I need to meet with Entrefacado Blathner.

Right.

I disrobe and jump into the pool.

Swimming, I think about the innovations of craft. How when they are documented on paper, or on the screen, or related in secondhand accounts, they are lost. That finding the legacy is reading between the lines. Acting cannot be transmitted in documents or lectures, but in seeing performance and playing in the vernacular of the age. That is why I will never again read a script. Literally unliterary. I breaststroke. I butterfly. I hold air and expel it all to sink toward the bottom to lie motionless beneath it all. Ten tame tadpoles tucked tightly in a thin tall tin. The waiting in water is what I wish to want as I wish to wash my Irish wristwatch. Seventy-eight, seventy-nine, eighty. I wonder, which wristwatches are Swiss wristwatches? Keeping customers content creates kingly profits. Bigger business isn't better business, but better business brings bigger rewards. I wonder what would happen if I breathed, and I take in a little water and imagine myself drinking it in. I almost choke. When I rise to the surface, I'm tired and spent, and I lift myself out of the pool.

Blathner reclines in a lounge chair, in polyester trousers and jacket. He has sunglass inserts in his eyeglasses and he's reading a fat stack of paper.

Disgusting, he says, putting a sheet of paper down under my ass as I sit in the chair next to him. He plugs a rubber pad into his phone and gives me a stylus.

I sign my name on the pad. Al fresco bodies make you uncomfortable?

This is retroactive, he says. What's this about you and Lucia doing Privation Therapy in Canada?

Yeah. Tomorrow. Jealous?

You can't go.

I can't not go.

You're contractually obligated to do a dryer sheets commercial tomorrow. I piggybacked it onto this film deal. You've signed over all of your time for the shoot. You're a burglar who breaks in to a suburban home and then decides to steal the sheets instead of the jewelry. The sheets are the softest sheets you've ever felt.

I give Blathner permission to go with us to Saskatchewan. I tell him it's 25 below there.

I'm amending the script and I don't have time. Plus, you can't go. His eyes wander back to the paper.

Without notice, he grabs the pathetic bouquet of flowers on the table next to him and throws them in my face.

I wave in his face. Do you ever tire of pushing people toward mediocrity?

Toward money?

I notice Blathner's neck is red. Where does it end? I say. It looks like he has collar rash. He has those zits that people get when their pores are clogged. It looks like it hurts. Does it hurt? I ask.

Every day hurts more than the last, he says. Just do what you're told.

I need to do what needs to be done, I say.

No, you don't.

I bring along with me the intensity that is associated with my temperament. I cannot do any less.

You know, Lucia is afraid you might be less than dedicated to her—to this whole thing.

She's afraid of herself, I say. She's afraid to give of herself to the point of insecurity. I'm not asking for anything unrealistic. When Lucia smiles, I want her to earn it. When she cries, I want it to hurt. Right now, she's going through the motions.

She loves you, son.

I never asked for that. I just wanted to be friends.

With friends like you—

And she's not the easiest person to love.

And you?

I am the laurel wreath on the brow of summer, I say.

That was good, Blathner says. How do you know this stuff already?

The Brute is an animal, I say. We went over all these lines while everyone was eating doughnuts and talking about how they waste their time consuming low media.

The door to the pool house opens and the PA gives me the OK. I see a rustling in the bushes and the youngster's bandana amidst the leaves. I get up and thank Blathner for his time. Cetaphil, I say. Dab it on every day, first-thing and last-thing. Towel it off. It clears up everything rightly over time. Do this or our relationship will suffer. You'll thank me later.

I'll thank you when this film's over and we get us some money.

You know what? I say. You'd be a believable Lucia's Father if you just kind of tidied up a bit.

I don't play.

Because even though I'm naked right here in front of you, you still can't see me.

Yeah, about that.

The youngster, camera in hand, acts like he's fixing a cable taped to the wall behind the bush.

I dress. Something like a Canadian tuxedo, but a little swankier. Pearl buttons and platform shoes. It occurs to me I need a heavy scarf. I look through the shelves. The scarf is thick and wide, heavy knit, cyan, almost a sweater. No one will miss it. I wrap it around my neck and almost get lost in front of the mirror. The Rolls should be here.

I stop by my lounge to throw three Poilly Fuissé bottles into my tote and I look at the oysters unshucked on the ice. I dump them into a trash bag with ice and the shucker, and put that under a stack of hand towels in the tote. Upstairs at Lucia's dressing room, she is packing. I ask her to bring enough makeup for both of us. She has leggings, T-shirts, frilly underwear, yoga pants, a sari, a leather jacket, Spanx, two big floppy hats, a parka. She finishes packing.

I take one of her bags and she takes the other, and I remind her Milo said to pack light. Milo will give us scrubs and trainers.

I did pack light, she says, and I don't care. I just got all this stuff from wardrobe. I'm certainly not going to leave it here.

Oysters? I raise the tote. Wine? I have to prove it to her by opening the bag and pushing the hand towels to the side.

Later, she says. We rattle down the stairs.

At the back of the compound, there's a wooden fence adjacent to a neighbor's house. Without waiting, I jump it. She throws me the bags and she follows them, scaling the wooden slats with not a little difficulty. It feels freer as we run limping under the weight of our bags through the grass and let ourselves out into the front yard of the house behind the compound. We're on the street. Palms are waving overhead. We walk a ways and see the white Rolls wheeling around the corner. I wave and the car drives toward us a bit slower than I would like. The driver steps out and we don't wait for him to help us as we open the door and stuff ourselves and our bags in on the sidewalk side. The driver's jacket is too tight. He smells of Cool Ranch Doritos.

Do it, I yell.

Whoa, whoa, whoa, says the driver. Okay. He shuffles back to his side of the car and gets in. You two in a hurry?

We don't want to miss our flight, Lucia says.

As we settle in and the car banks, I gaze out the window and fix on the sunny beams of heat. Lucia grabs my arm to fix my attention. I've been reading up on P.T., she says.

Anything good? I ask.

It's a little weird.

We turn onto Los Feliz Boulevard. The sun reflects off the windshields of the cars. There is a cloudless sky. The driver whistles to make it seem like he's not listening.

Weird good?

I'm not sure, she says. Sensory deprivation. Snow wallowing. Group grooming. Raw meat?

Just have an open mind, I say. Raw meat might be negotiable.

Raw meat's good, says the driver. Land sushi.

We pause and consider his part in our conversation. We do not respond. Lucia's hair is long and brown. It looks feathery, like it's been fluffed and filled-in with some kind of foundational product, then gingerly sprayed and lifted up so that it falls cleverly over the side of her face. We should start drinking, I say. I notice the driver looking in the rearview mirror often. I look back over my shoulder. I see nothing of note. What's back there? I ask.

Nothing, he says.

The Rolls has a bar—Gin, Jack, Campari, Captain, André, disaster. Lucia's phone chirps and vibrates violently. Turn it off, I say.

She glances at the phone in horror. Foster, she says.

Turn it off. I pour her a whiskey and soda. I hand it to her.

She turns it off. She breathes deeply. We could kill this film.

If we can't get our heads straight, the film won't matter, I say.

She puts her phone right on top of her bag. I clink myself some ice and give myself the luxury of ice water. It will strain my vocal cords sufficiently.

Who is Lucia? I ask. Tell me.

Lucia?

Yes, I say. You.

I'm a writer who acts.

What is it you love to act about?

That's a serious question? She frowns a bit.

I insist.

Okay, she says, I hate comedy. The kind of comedy where the characters address the camera. I hate sports—they seem like a continual replay of the same acts over and over again.

And love?

Brokenness. We are broken in so many different ways. Broken roles are the most important ones.

Brokenness emoted?

I love it when a character is destroyed—how that character finds some way of bouncing back.

An example? I ask. The car slows to a crawl. We're on the freeway.

The best role I've ever played was Mathilde the Bouffon.

Not buffoon? I ask.

A bouffon is different than a buffoon. Mathilde had long dark hair. She constantly had her head in her hands. But not stupid—she says—a bouffon is closer to a farceur or jester—Mathilde would sit motionless, absently gazing into space. She would finger her fingers as if she were counting. The kind of places where Mathilde would sit would be courtrooms. As Lucia speaks, her eyes throw wide. White collar cases, or political meetings. Often where the outcome of the cases would permanently change the course of the lives of the working-class poor. Mathilde would mumble phrases, but with her mouth closed like she had a psychic power to speak without speaking. She would connect in her mumbled phraseology with the attention of the privileged individuals in the court—those who were attempting to further their careers, but who couldn't because of legal trouble. Her own brokenness was to match the brokenness of the helpless people being disenfranchised. Mathilde would interfere with the proceedings by supplying a big fat earworm that always forced the attention on her. But she would avoid eye contact. She would keep her face down. And then, at that moment she would look up and around at everyone in the room and produce an oversized sketchpad, and do charcoal drawings of everyone there. But she would not get very far, because, inevitably, those in power would stop her. She always asked, But why? Why can I not draw? Who is it hurting? How does my art offend? I mean you no harm. Mathilde's job was to produce insecurity.

How would she hold her chin? I ask.

Like this. No, maybe it was more like this.

Then where would she put it?

Lucia drops her forehead slightly and gazes up at me. She has tousled her hair so that it streams down the sides of her face, and she gives a petty grumble and breathes in through her nose.

Was this theater or film?

Theater, she says. That kind of action would never fly in a film. For it to be in a film, a hero would have to take interest in Mathilde, and, through some plot contrivance, transform Mathilde into some kind of better person with acceptable credulity; Mathilde making everyone question their confidence would not be enough. It's too uncomfortable.

Did it play in New York?

Chicago.

So, no one saw it.

Acting for acting's sake.

New York is a necropoly, Los Angeles an apocalopolis, but Chicago? I take a drink and the water is frigid but weak. I can't bring myself to drink the bottom shelf stuff in the car. But I do maintain I will open the wine on the plane.

She takes a drink.

While we drive, I edge out onto the edge of my seat and slump down so that she kind of looks over a bit wondering where I'm going. She takes out a Polaroid camera. We need to document this, she says. In case we go missing.

I look in at her down my nose and angle my head. The lighting in the car is top notch. I keep my mouth somewhat open to draw her in. She takes one photo from way up near the ceiling of the car. I'm slumping, derelict.

We're closing in on the airport, the driver says.

Lucia laughs because I keep making my face ugly and impenetrable. She knows I'm trying to ruin the shots and she won't take a picture until she can get a good one, so I'm stopping her from everything. It makes her scrunch up her nose to steel herself.

Ask me a politically incorrect question, I say.

Religion or politics?

Religion.

Alright, let me think. She threatens with the camera up over her face. Okay, she says, I got it. What, in your opinion keeps people from believing in God? Selfishness, ambition, science?

Fear.

Fear of others?

Fear that everything believed will be proven wrong. The fact that they are not smart enough, strong enough, rich enough, beautiful enough, unique enough, talented enough to have created for themselves their own worlds. That everything they have done amounts to nothing. Fear that their worlds have not been created for their glory. That they will be held accountable for that which they had done and not done. That God is not into them for their sakes, but for His own. Fear from not knowing.

You believe in this God?

Yes.

You know this?

Yes.

Proof?

None. I have only my experience. I do not know the same thing you do not know.

How then?

The epiphany. The flash of light. Everyone has had one. Everyone chooses a response.

You're joking.

I've heard that before. Camus writes about his epiphany in *The Stranger*. He is out in the sun in the Mediterranean. The sun, instead of blinding him, makes him see more. He enters into crisis. It causes him to kill, or at least causes Camus's character to kill. And then there's Saul of Tarsus. Saul sees the light, has his epiphany, then goes blind. Camus's response is to become an existentialist. Saul of Tarsus becomes the apostle Paul. Choices are made. Who should be more afraid, the one who chooses self over others, or the one who becomes adopted by God? Paul's name changes, he's all in, but The Stranger kills and is locked up.

Now you're a Christian?

I know.

What about the murder? Hypocrisy? War? Intolerance? Racism? Hate? These are all hallmarks of religion.

Should fear of that keep us apart from the Master of the Universe? God's violence is a problem, and yet, and yet, these problems are all hallmarks of atheism as well.

Lucia snaps me with the Polaroid. She uses the flash, although it's unnecessary, and it pops. I'm dizzy and I reel a bit. It catches me by surprise.

I look down and the ice has melted in my cup and the water is sloshing around with the movement of the car. I pour it over my head, tears in my eyes. I wipe them away. We're here, I say.

The driver drives us up to the curb and gets out and puts our bags down next to us. I thank him and buffet his shoulder and hand him a bottle of Poilly Fuissé. Tell no one about us, I say.

He takes it and does a double take.

That's good shit, I say.

He mumbles something under his breath and I hand him a fifty. He laughs as if the joke's on him and I only slightly regret giving the bottle away, but then convince myself I did the right thing. Maybe sober will be good. There'll be hardship in Canada.

The driver gets on his phone and looks back at us as he drives away. I turn around to look behind me. It's hotter out than I remember it being. I stand together with Lucia and stare into the abyss of the airport terminal. I have Lucia's duffel, and my tote of wine and oysters, and she's wearing a purse and dark sunglasses, pulling her roller. We begin in on the terminal. We check in and our tickets are a go. First Class as far as we can, then a bus on wings to Prince Albert Airport. They take Lucia's bags, and we turn around. She asks me if we should really go through with this.

I'm thinking I should say a flea and a fly flew up in a flue, but I say I thought I thought of thinking of thanking you.

I need to get drunker, she says.

I tell her we'll drink plenty on the plane.

We walk toward security and I feel the feeling I feel before a show when there is no going back, when I must embrace the beast. It is scandalous, violent. It is a myth that I can stay in control. My spine tingles under the weight of fear. I switch to carry the bag under a different arm. My hands bristle, I have not exercised enough today. The swimming was insufficient.

As we approach the security line, in the corner of my eye I catch the shape of a man in a threadbare suit and a black cape bent down over his cane. He wears a fierce and gentle profile, and he lopes as he shuffles along, and he's making his way toward us. I am transfixed. His tie is heavy knotted. His knuckles are gnarled. The knees in his pants are worn out. This side of his face is like tree bark. His walking cane is expensive, as if a rod of marble was bookended in pewter. He is attractive but not handsome.

Hey you! He says with his arm up. You! He strikes out with his cane. He scoots toward us. Lucia grabs my arm.

Yes? Lucia says.

He gets within striking distance and hits me in the leg with his cane. It does nothing to me. He acts as if I know him.

What are you doing here? He asks.

I tell him it's inconsequential.

He looks at Lucia. How dare you! Here, open this envelope. Take it and look inside and then tell me what you're doing here in this place.

Who are you? I ask.

The Producer, he says. Take the envelope. Take it!

I look at him hard. I don't read, I say.

You can't read? He looks at Lucia. He can't read?

He can read, she says.

I take the envelope and listen to it. There is no ticking. I hold it up to the light cans in that cavernous space and cannot discern anything discernable. I shrug and open it and there's nothing inside. Bystanders crane necks to hear what we're talking about. I notice there are two big guys in suits closing in from behind the Producer. Lizard people. Svelte.

That's right, the Producer says.

He looks to Lucia. He looks to me.

He swivels with an energy that is unlocatable. He is taut and light on his feet. He looks around the airport arrogantly while I size him up. It's as if he's used to being looked at, as if he has never had anything to be ashamed of. But he looks off balance, like one push with a finger would make him topple.

I get a tap on my shoulder and there's a familiar voice. Hey baby.

It's Avril. Lucia drops my arm. Avril hugs. We hug. She asks if I'm all ready to go. She sees Lucia and it registers for all of us.

Us? Lucia asks.

The man shakes his head. Not in my terminus.

He takes the envelope back and puts it in his pocket. He grabs Lucia by the hand and she seems to contemplate her future as an actor. She's more than happy to walk with him. This was ill-conceived, she says. They begin to walk away. Avril grabs Lucia's hand and I've been had. As they walk Lucia throws her head back. It's like a coin in a wishing well, she says. The three of them start walking.

As they go, Avril smiles and turns. It's almost time for the dailies, she says. Then she mouths at me, I got this. They walk away arm-in-arm, holding up the Producer, and I look around. They've left me thinking about what to do at the security check with my oysters and my wine.

I stand in wonderment. The suits are still over there, but they've gotten much closer. I sit down in the middle of the terminal and open up my tote to console myself with luncheon. I get up and walk over to a condiment bar on the edge of an airport restaurant. I take some lemon slices. The lizard people edge in and stand next to me looking on. I go back to my luncheon on the floor. I shuck oysters and heavily apply lemon juice. I eat all of them with relish. They are like diamond jelly.

When I finish, I try a little experiment. I leave the spent oyster shells and the empty bottle of wine and my trash on the floor and walk away. The suits shift attention. I walk toward the terminal exit. One of them scoops up my stuff and puts it in a trash bin, then grabs Lucia's bags. The other follows me. Now they are both following. The gravity of the situation depresses my mind. There is no fighting it. I turn around and walk back to the men and introduce myself. I ask for a ride. They look like they cannot laugh, like they lack the capacity. We walk the interminable walk out of the terminal and down the curb to their black Chevy Suburban, idling in the red zone.

In the car, I'm told to ride in the middle row. Jim drives and Neal sits behind me, making conversation difficult. The windows are heavily tinted. Six thick thistle sticks. Six thick thistles stick. Top chopstick shops stock top chopsticks. My shoes are blue with yellow stripes and green stars on the front.

We drive along until we get to the freeway, then we stop. Why is the freeway the slowest place to drive? I ask.

Silence.

Why do we drive on parkways and park on driveways?

Neal asks, Is that Seinfeld?

No.

I think it is, he replies.

It isn't.

Yes, I think it is.

It is, says Jim.

No, it's not, I say. It's not, because I didn't give a catchphrase.

What's that?

No, it's not What's that? It's What's the deal with that? Or something like that, I think.

Oh, says Neal.

I tap Jim's shoulder. Have you two ever considered relationship therapy?

Silence.

Have you two ever considered therapy?

Never.

Have you two ever considered?

There's no relationship.

Ever?

No.

I'll tell you about it.

Do we have to talk? Jim asks.

Don't worry, I say, you can just sit there.

In Privation Therapy for couples, I say, all of our defenses are to be stripped away. For this, there is a requirement for us to leave our familiar environs. We would be relocated to a cold weather environment. We would work to have our temperatures acclimate to the snow. The goal of this would be that we would become snow borne. Then we would groom each other, exfoliate each other's skin. We would comb each other's hair, sharpen each other's nails. Rub each other's feet, hands, and thighs. We would coat each other with oils and then bathe in an icy river. Then, to heat ourselves up we would go out into the forest and scream, and run, and chase each other, and attempt to become lost. We would look for shelter. When we found something more comfortable than full exposure, we would huddle together and then accuse each other of all the things we are ourselves guilty of. Then the ones on the receiving end of this would forgive the others of their perceived offenses. That would be day one. That would be initiation. The rest of the night we would group-compose a song narrating that day's adventure. And so on. A week of this.

The three of us, Neal says, keeping a straight, hardened expression, only occasionally turning his neck to take in some piece of freeway data important for the mission.

It could just be you two, I say. I wouldn't have to go. Unless you want me to? Do you? Do you want me to go with?

There is no response. Time passes.

I think about how walking is better than riding. When you walk your basic human electronic wiring fires and the spark of life ignites. It is like the recharging of a battery. Voltage, so to speak. If I walk long enough my body does not want to stop walking.

It begins to operate on some sort of self-perpetuating cycle. The more I walk, the more I can walk, the more I want to walk, and so on.

Stuck on the freeway in the middle row of seats, air conditioning blasting, I begin to compose a romantic relationship with walking in my head. I remember it fondly. I want to return to the time when walking walked me well. When I walk I do well. I wander and I wonder. I ponder and I pander. I can breathe and think and dream and desire and feel and love. I finally focus. I feel more like fathering ideas than foundering at dead ends or fingering lockless keys.

The men in the car keep their eyes forward. Sure, their heads swivel and their eyes flash and scan, but it continually appears that all of their attention is facing straight ahead. They are straightforward people.

For an observationalist, hitches can be misleading. When walking, sure, there are pains that manifest themselves. These are physical pains, but they are more specifically manifestations of the heart. When the heart feels pain, the heart reminds the body that the body is in a state of pain. Take a man who walks with a hitch. When his heart is light, the hitch is forgotten. He moves with grace. His impediments are benign. The great struggle is to lighten one's load, to feel unencumbered, to hurt no more. When one hitches, all one can see are the outward signs of a heart in pain. The man walks with a hitch, he wobbles, I am unconcerned with him, I only see him jerk and stagger. But if I examine my own heart, I know that there, there is the pain. The pain of having missed so many opportunities that I should have taken hold of. The pain of having closed myself off from my brother, stonewalling any opportunity we might have of becoming closer because of my various rules about what I will do and what I won't do to make peace, or right the wrongs, or help us heal. For example, my brother has never asked forgiveness or sought amends for the things he did to me when we were little—holding me down and dropping gobs of spit from overhead, attempting to land them in my mouth. Me, keeping my lips closed, breathing out of my nose, holding my breath so that the spit would not enter my mouth, him spitting over and over, dropping balls of that rank-smelling fluid so that it collects on my closed lips, so that I have to shake it off my face and I can only breathe from my nose. Him taking up a BB gun and running toward me to shoot me from close range. Me always retreating, trying to gain distance or a gap from him. Him, when being left to watch me at home when our parents had left us alone, forcing me to spend that entire amount of time—what seemed like ten hours at a stretch—shut up in my room on the bottom pallet of a twin bunkbed, shut in for so long that I pee myself, and the urine soaks irretrievably into the mattress, staining the sheets and creating those frustrated coffee-colored whorls of piss stains on the mattress-top forever.

These are the kinds of pain that I think of when examining my heart, thinking about what walking is. Those causes that cause one to limp are the kinds of causes which matter. They are from a very real place of pain in the heart and can only truly manifest themselves truthfully outwardly. When I think of them, I think of any kind of pain that could cause my body to limp, hitch, drag, fumble, fail, tremor, writhe. Any of these can be conjured up because they are at that moment more to me than any mechanical representation that I might add to my stock gestures.

The car continues on. Black bug's blood. Black bug's blood. Black bug's blood. It appears that these men have never considered the possibility that therapy may do them good.

So, no to P.T.? I ask.

We've arrived, Neal says.

Jim says, It's been a pleasure.

We are back at film HQ. I exit the car and extend hard cash to leave them a tip. Their stares are hard to the point of cliché. I leave a fifty on the seat.

I walk from the curb toward the McVilla, surrounded by trucks and trailers. I see that the movie furniture has been struck for the day, and the PA attaches herself to my side to tell me about all that has happened. I was there, I say. I ask where Zozotte is. Zozotte is in the lounge playing some sort of first-person shooter.

I enter the house and approach the room. She is sitting next to her variety box of Pop Rocks and a crew member who wears a Dodgers cap and a Lakers jersey.

Did you get a part? I ask.

She continues playing, focusing with intensity, but some difficulty, on the screen.

Still angry?

Her lips are quivering and her eyes flicker with activated light. She grasps the controller in a rigid manner. Zozotte wears a gray wife beater and baggy stonewashed jeans over black Vans showing her ankles. She has this impossible kind of vertical pony tail sticking straight up from the middle of her head like a pith.

I was never mad, she says. Whatever you've concocted in your head is your business.

How's your acting?

I'm still stuck doing the play.

The crew member next to her acts like an extra.

Are you doing the dailies? She asks.

Are you? I ask.

Of course, she says. Are you crazy?

The crew member laughs.

I tell Zozotte I am impressed she's still here.

Not all of us have work, she says.

Have you spoken with Foster?

Are you crazy-crazy?

The crew member slaps his knee.

Blathner?

Never thought of that, she says.

As her shoulders negotiate the free space of the electronic world, I feel her need to be free. She giggles in a forced way as she plays. Sometimes she taps her feet. Other times, she hits the couch with a loose hand. She is in no way ugly. She does all this under the guise of ignoring me.

And what is my problem with Zozotte? She has seen me steal from a tip jar. I swapped a one for a five right in front of a barista while Zozotte was watching. And she has seen me rub my crotch—not scratch it—while fixated on the triangle shape made between the inner thighs and pudenda of that same barista in her black semitransparent leggings. She has witnessed me clear my throat, cough up phlegm and swallow it because of its comforting connection to my own personal flavor. She saw me scratch my asshole and smell it. She saw me trying to trip a little kid just to watch him fall helplessly on his face. She has watched as I took outgoing mail from a mailbox in passing as we walked by it and put it directly into a trash can. Zozotte knows that I do not have the birthdays of either of my parents, nor my brother, memorized. She once watched through a crack in the door as I stared at myself in the mirror and admired my own facial expressions for a full thirty-five minutes, without saying a word—a continuous gesture and performance that inspired in me an elated happiness for that entire period. I am a bad person and she knows it, and because she knows it and I know she knows it, I am attached to her. It may even be this very thing that has caused her not to entirely and completely break free from me. I do not know.

I leave her to her game and walk in through a series of doors and out through the back of the house so that I can change. I get to my room and no one is there. I grab the phone that Blathner got me. I check, and all my phone numbers have been inputted. I sit on a Persian rug in the middle of the floor and begin to breathe. The seething sea ceaseth, and thus the seething sea sufficeth us. My legs stretch out in front of me and I stretch my hands over and atop my feet. I throw my shoes off to the side and lay back on the floor.

I phone the therapist, Milo. It rings and rings and he answers.

He stammers. I can hear a helicopter chopping behind his voice. Where are you?

I'm not going to make it, I say.

We've prepared this amazeballs session for you, bro. This will be your life-changing kiss with wilderness.

I missed the flight.

I don't want to hear that, he says. Milo seems fun, but he is not a generous person. It is why he is a good therapist. He is merciless and relentless. He has been waiting at the airport for some time now. He will come at me. He will hunt me down. No doubt. He is my only connection to my brother.

Why aren't you talking, brah? he asks.

I'm apologizing, I say. Now what?

He begins talking.

I hang up.

I get up and approach the armoire. The PA has filled the armoire with beautiful things. I riffle through them to find something fresh. There is a wide Panama hat, and a vintage polyester shirt with clever lapels, and high-waisted slacks, and some Italian boots. By the time I dress and moisturize it is leave time. In the hall, I ask the closest person—a millennial hefting a large metal bar—where the dailies are.

II.

Outside the bungalow, in a big white tent set up over the opposite yard, there are about a hundred beach chairs facing an oversized projector screen. The chairs are almost all occupied. I walk forward and a PA says hello, and motions me toward the front to sit next to Lucia, Brutus, Avril, Zozotte, and the Producer. Jim and Neal stand by. I see Oliver over to the side, angry, taking photographs, turtle necking. People are eating popcorn. Foster sees me and steps up to the front. He's wearing a maroon wool sweater and corduroy pants and chukka boots. He takes the mic.

Everyone settle down, he says. Thank you—thank you—We shot a lot today and it's all because of your hard work—This isn't a true set of dailies, because it extends out over a longer period than 24 hours—but this is a substantial portion of what we were able to get in the last thirty-six hours—Here we go.

The footage begins. The colors are washed out. It's grainy. There's an hour of shots around North Hollywood. Interesting angles. Insalubre is a speck in some of the frames. Insalubre looks pathetic and small.

Then there are shots of the compound. Mood work. The hedges. Insalubre and Brutus exchange violence. The cuts are quick. Comic book framing. Brutus is pregnant with strain. They fight it out on a patch of dirt. Both are broken.

Now we are inside Foster's trailer—interior room—claustrophobic. Insalubre and Lucia have a heart-to-heart. She looks frantic, aimless, ravished. She's unable to keep up with the conversation. The desperation is apparent.

Lucia and Insalubre walk arm-in-arm. What they say appears important. Insalubre has complicated hair.

Insalubre swims naked. His skin is perfect.

Insalubre and Blathner are poolside. They lean toward and away from each other like they're dancing. Insalubre is bludgeoned with flowers.

Insalubre and Lucia run away from the house. They appear as if they have no experience at running.

Insalubre and Lucia chat in the Rolls and take photos. They laugh and cry. There is an awkward imbalance in each shot. These are happy times.

Insalubre and Lucia are outside the airport. They are dwarfed by the overwhelming size of the building.

Insalubre, Lucia, and the Producer are inside the airport terminal. The shots are too didactic. The Producer plays it too thin. What is the point? Bystanders crowd the scene.

Jim and Neal leave the airport with Insalubre captive. There they are again inside the SUV. There's a lot of melancholy sitting, looking straight ahead. It is a place where boredom has its place. It seems to work.

Lots of B-roll of Los Angeles. Swimming pools, palm trees, heat radiating. The dailies end.

Foster stands and turns back toward us. Of course, he says, wrapping it up, we'll record the voiceover later—Be ready tomorrow for another full day—Be ready to go early—I cannot thank you enough.

Blathner takes me by the arm and walks me out of the tent. This script is as necessary as a unicorn fart, he says.

You look better, I say. I see the neck's on the mend.

Thanks. There's an esthetician on set. She's smokin'. Let's go.

He walks me off the property toward his Chrysler Sebring. It's waiting for us down the block from the set. Around the neighborhood, people are arriving home from work. The street is coming back to life. We get in the car.

Where? I ask.

Glendale—you know. We gotta be ready first thing in the morning so we can shoot.

I pop open the cooler behind the seat. Bartles and Jaymes? I ask. They still make this?

Gimme one of those, he says. He motors the car off down the street and puts on a baseball cap that has a logo for a sailing merchandise company on it. I give him a bottle and he pops the lid. I hate the freeways, he says. It's all about the side streets.

We drive. It is an uncomfortable series of stops and starts, and I am not at rest. The flood of air and the violence of the potholed road keeps my mind untethered. He holds a cigarette in his left hand and a wine cooler between his legs. His hand hangs over the front of the steering wheel like an alpha dog's. His phone is jacked into the stereo, so I have to listen to him talk to his assistant. Then he talks to a go-between, then a producer for the commercial.

We have to do this in a four-hour window, he says.

The guy on the other phone says, no way, six hours.

We can't, Blathner says. We're not able to stay longer. Gargon shoots at noon.

Blathner hangs up. This is shit. He makes another call and can't get through. What do you think, Gargon?

And if the shoot came to us? I say.

Hold on, he says.

The phone purrs. He answers. He throws his cigarette onto Rowena Avenue and unplugs the phone from the speaker.

Yeah, he says, yeah. Okay. Interesting. You cocksucker. No? Me? You. Me? Okay, bye.

You know, Milo's not backing down, he says. No one's gonna be able to stop him from coming onto set tomorrow and getting in your kitchen.

I have nothing to hide.

And what is that? he asks.

I think about it. It would be good to know. I have a history of paranoid schizophrenia, I say. I'm on medically prescribed Abilify, Fluoxetine, and Clonazepam.

Is that all, he says.

I am able to carry on a conversation without spontaneously mentioning psychotic delusions or hallucinations. I have never birthed any children that have been given away to strangers without my knowledge. I cannot hear the voice of my phantom daughter crying out for the $857.39 that I had always intended on giving to her mother. My focus on work is much improved. I am eating healthy. I do not believe anyone is actively trying to poison me by way of food or coffee, and I have maintained this view for the past ten years. Robbing a convenience store has never occurred to me. I am altogether free from my bouts of delirium tremens, hypertension, bilateral lumbar radiculopathy, arm and shoulder pain, stress, onset incontinence, and constipation. My experimentation with Enablex, Lisinopril-HCTZ, Lortab, metaformin hydrochloride, Miralax, and Omeprazole has decreased to negligible, making me able to claim freedom from illicit drug use. I am down to one or two Gauloises a day and three tiny cappuccinos. I've been able to silence the reverberating pangs of perceived adolescent sexual abuse in my head as I have washed myself seven times in the Los Angeles River. Though the concept of washing away the evil is ever-present in my life, I am drawn to organized religion as a stable rock upon which to build the unwrecked from the wrecked. If I am love-sick, I can kiss the picture of the one I love and feel satisfied. And if I kiss a picture of myself, I can receive and give a kind of satisfaction. It's unsanitary, yes, but it's profoundly efficient. I am rich, though I am poor. I want to nap, but I cannot bring myself to the point of rest. I imagine myself sleeping and then think about how much work it would take for me to reengage after sleeping.

I ask Blathner if he will protect me from Milo, when Milo comes for me.

I'll do what I can, he says.

I thank him and we proceed down streets at an unconscionably slow speed.

Tell me again what we're doing? I ask. Dryer sheets make sleek feet meet neat fit sheets.

Blathner is not one to question the posterity of an action. He is driving me to the money. He tells me that this will pass, and I run my hands through my hair and imagine what things could have been like if I was more adamant. I tell Blathner I want to go scout the set for the film shoot. I tell him there's a ton of time before the commercial tomorrow morning, and that it's important for the process. When he balks, I say we might as well shoot the scene tonight.

Uh, yeah?

That we should fire up the crew.

He is tired. He deplores me. And yet he wants all of this done so as to collect his fee.

I tell him the dryer sheets thing will not be anything if I cannot get back to Insalubre. With his phone back up to his ear, he pulls over at a gas station convenience store. I will leak, he says.

I sit. I watch the lot and the pumping of gas. There is a pent-up boredom and a transitory vibration in those on their way in and out and back into their cars. I notice a father leave his maroon Camaro next to a pump and walk toward the store. I step out and sidle over to the passenger side of the other car. There is a reedy little girl sitting in the passenger seat with her door propped open and her leg hanging out, her foot lilting side to side.

Have you ever thought of running away? I ask.

She leans out the door and shades her eyes. She looks at me as if I'd just killed her turtle. She says, It never crossed my mind.

Have you ever wanted something so bad that nothing was going to stop you?

She has an angry chin, but it is also a thoughtful chin. You mean like how I want to pay my rent?

Something bigger than that, I say. Is that your father?

She laughs a stifled laugh. Something like that, she says.

She is captive like I am captive. What if you could run away and join the circus? I ask.

I'd consider it, she says.

I tell her that making a movie is the closest thing to the circus that there is.

Like, how would you know?

Making a movie's also like going to summer camp, I say. It's really the only way to get to know others in a purely social way; the only way to be a part of a loving, caring community.

She's picking at her fingernails. And you have some kind of way for me to do this?

Yes.

She doesn't really care. What is it about a person that makes them want to stay the same? I cannot relate. I cannot stay the same. I am uncomfortable as I am. I hate who I used to be. What is better than to become something new?

Circus camp doesn't sound interesting, she says.

Perhaps not, perhaps not. I look up. Here comes your father, I say.

She laughs again. The stench of gasoline is nauseating. Yeah.

Later, I say. I walk.

The father takes the fuel dock off the car and puts it back in its cradle. She slams the door violently and reclines her seat back and she puts her hands behind her head to get comfortable.

I look up and Blathner's walking toward me, readjusting his belt with one hand, pressing his phone to his ear with the other. He says to me, A crew will meet us in Glendora.

This is good news. I tell him to put Insalubre in the trunk.

What?

Insalubre insists.

You're gonna kill yourself, kid.

The trunk of a Chrysler Sebring is not as dark as one might expect. As Blathner drives there are the reverberations of an epic Philip Glass instrumental piece muffled through the speakers in the car's upholstery. As I settle in, I decide to change for the scene. I brought a pair of Chinos which I struggle on. I roll up the legs and take off my socks and put my shoes back on. I don't know why Blathner has an old necktie back here, but I use it as a belt. As I struggle with a button up Oxford, I begin to meld into something more vital. Character is the borrowing of bones. Character is the armature to build a life upon and the bones are borrowed from life. I stretch and I center myself and imagine myself as the only life in this scene. The waiting is endless. I open myself up to the waiting. I accept it as the only way through. My emotional memory is thin. There is an inescapable barrier between me and the fresh air. I must kick my way through. I turn and find a comfortable angle in which to lie. We continue on.

After an interminable number of stops and starts, the car tires make dull rolling crunches as we move over gravel. We come to a stop. I feel Blathner's door shut and his footsteps walking away from the car. I switch positions and resettle on my back. The tension heightens my senses. My mind races with the single-minded purpose necessary for the scene. I can hear the give and the take of voices outside and a pause and then more exchanged conversation. When it dies down, I hear doors shutting and a group of footsteps walking back and forth on the gravel. I wait. There is only a faint smell of car exhaust and that pungent gasoline smell, and though it is night, some streams of light come through the cracks in the trunk. The rhythm begins to feel good. I can feel it gathering inside. I begin to rock and press upon myself and something begins to take shape.

Insalubre kicks at the rear seat wall between the trunk and the rear seat. It is stable, but then it gives way a little. One kick after another he kicks the plastic and it begins to fracture. All at once, his foot goes through the stuffing in the back of the seat and he pulls out some fluffy padding with his hands. Insalubre goes to work on the framing for the seat, bending and breaking the weakest parts, and kicking small pieces of plastic. As he kicks the seat into bits, he hears a loud dull roar outside gathering at a distance. Bells ring and the adrenaline hits him full on. He finally rips through the back seat and pulls his body through. The top is up on the car, so he kicks his way out from the inside, his shoulders down on the back seat. He's moving so quickly that he easily tears through the convertible top and pushes his way out the car onto its hood. When Insalubre feels fresh air, he looks left and right. He turns like a madman and runs toward the train tracks unheeded. What is it that makes a madman brave?

Blathner sees this and shouts, but it makes no difference. Insalubre makes it to the tracks just ahead of the train and lays down between the rails on his back with his face up to the sky. Straight away the train rampages over him, covering his view in its mechanized bustle, car after car, metal scraping and solid pressure, turn after turn as steel wheels roll on.

To sit in solemn silence in a dull, dark, dock, in a pestilential prison, with a life-long lock, awaiting the sensation of a short, sharp, shock, from a cheap and chippy chopper on a big black block. The train passes over Insalubre and he wets himself. It's not so much from being scared, but it is the control required to stay flat for that long. The train tries to travel flat over Insalubre's front out of Glendale. He grounds himself to stay alive fast to the rocks in the middle of the tracks. It is a massive undertaking.

The train passes on and he slowly gets to his feet. Insalubre sees Milo. Milo wears a headband, puffy snow jacket, shorts, and tall hiking boots. His socks are pulled up to his knees. He rushes to Insalubre and embraces him with a towel. He is aware of the cameras and keeps looking at them. The two of them walk to an enormous tour bus chugging and vibrating, parked in the gravel parking lot.

You are absolutely catatonic, he says.

I need Lucia.

Milo takes Insalubre into the bus and into the bus's shower and strips him down and turns the spigot and its temperature to cold.

How'd you get past Blathner? Insalubre asks.

He was on his phone, Milo says. Plus, I'm clever. He's so weaksauce.

The phone is how you can be somewhere and nowhere all in one place.

And Lucia?

Are you sure?

Yes, I'd like to speak with her.

The shower is frigid. The bus is comfortable as there is wall-to-wall carpet. There are pillows and throws on the couch. Milo appears not to be able to handle the ever-present psychic energy of the always rolling cameras. He gets weirded out. Here's a prescription, he says.

Read it aloud, I say.

```
Brah,
    Even if it is not convenient, it is nec-
essary for Entrefacado Blathner to be cradled
in the arms of a loved one every three hours.
The purpose of this is to reduce the amount
of aggressive and antihumanist ideations and
to promote attachments to human forms and
likenesses. This will result in better agent-
ing and better personhood.
        It's all about you,
        Milo Braxis, MFT.
```

All I want to do is talk to Lucia, I say.

I'll do what I can, he says.

That's all you can do.

He nods. Then there's nothing here for me. He leaves after glancing around at all the lenses stuck up at all kinds of angles. The youngster in the bandana knocks and enters immediately. He's talking to Foster on a hands-free device while he adjusts the rigging on the inside of the bus.

Insalubre says, Hi.

The youngster says, What's up.

Apart from all the cameras and the cords being taped up the wall, the inside of the bus looks very much like a bourgeois living room. It is one. At least it is as a cutaway. In the bedroom at the back of the bus there is a wardrobe full of clothes. I find a pair of black leathers and a seventies-era metal belt with links shaped like scallop shells. I put them on along with a beaded necklace and wrap a blanket over my shoulders and lounge on the couch, fooling with my hair, twisting it into braids, and forming the rest into a messy plait.

The youngster is fixated, attaching lights on one side of the room. He tells me he finds he can bounce the light off a disc over the top of the couch and against another wall. He says, Check. He leaves.

Lucia enters. Her mascara is running and she's wearing a silvery couture party dress and she rushes onto me and falls down on her knees.

What is there to say?

You're right, I cannot say, she says, nodding, but that's not what I want right now. She gazes off as if open and sympathetic. Try again to tell me.

My brother, I say, I want to tell you about him.

I'm here, she says.

I begin, We're in a rocky field on clay and motley stones. Him on a hillock. I throw a rock at him with genuine hate. It's an impossible Hail Mary and somehow it flies up and all the way across the field and hits him in the right eye. He falls forward cupping his hand to his eye. The rest of the day he is crying.

Now I'm holding my bike up on its back wheel to protect myself from him. He taunts me. I'll shoot you, he says. He squares the BB gun. No, don't. Come on, don't shoot. It's a real gun. I'll shoot. No, don't, I'm serious. He shoots and a BB hits me in the shin. My flesh catches it and holds it in a burning cave of blood. It is there to this day.

He's high behind the tool shed. What are you doing? I say. Don't tell mom, he says. I should tell Mother. Don't do it. Why'd you quit school? Don't do it. Mom already knows, he says. He says she knows but cannot do anything about it.

In the kitchen, Mother is in her nightgown frying eggs. He's hysterical. He edges past her to open the drawer and takes up a 14-inch chef's knife. I hate you—why don't you just leave me alone? Mother screams and starts crying out, put it away, put it away. He comes back at her. Yell at me one more time and I'll kill you.

Lucia tells me to stop. For your sake, stop.

I move off the couch and onto the floor. I take up a comb. I comb my own hair. I am fixated. I arrange my hair with combs. My brother sits in some place deep down within me. My hair is combed up.

I haven't done anything all day, I say. Pose with me.

Not in this dress.

Lucia walks to the back of the bus and goes through the compartments.

While I wait, I move into a Tripod, hands and head on the floor, knees tucked in. I hold it. I carried the married character over the barrier.

She returns, and so we can see each other eye to eye, she assumes the Tripod directly facing me. What do we do next? she asks.

The Air Chair, but we move to it slowly from Tripod to Broken Candlestick to Dazzler. Let's hold the Tripod. Do you like this?

I like.

We hold the Tripod, then we proceed.

She is fast enough and follows me through the motions, and though there is not so much room on the bus, we are able to proceed well through each pose, attempting to enter and exit each one, approaching each pose in a proficient way. I imagine an imaginary menagerie manager imagining managing an imaginary menagerie. Every other pose is about control, but the Dazzler is where you let it free. Bend low and whip your arms like a terrible storm.

Lucia grows tired, so she moves on, over to the couch. I spin and whip my arms. I draw myself out.

She speaks, and it is an opportunity for me to focus in order to hear. It is so comfortable for her to sit on the couch under a throw and psychologize.

Don't ignore me, she says.

Let me gather my thoughts, I say.

By all means.

I lay flat on the floor. I begin to be still to slow myself down and make my movements go at the speed of a sedentary pulse. She has me still and silent.

I tell her I am persecuted by my brother. That because of him I hide. I am mortified by the truth that I might never forgive him. That deep-down I am unable to forgive.

She asks if I'm acting, or if I'm lying, or if I'm stoned. From the floor looking up at her she looks so overbearing.

When I act, I say, and I'm always acting, my work is conceived in deception and pain.

She nods, And what could it be if you could let it go?

I don't think we'll ever know, I say.

I close my eyes to signify the end of the scene, but she does not move from the couch. I am stiff and make myself solid on the floor. After some time, she gets up and steps over me and leaves. The foreign authorities put Dorothy in an orange forest. Good blood, bad blood, good blood, bad blood, red blood, blue blood, red blood, blue blood. Black bug's blood. I again carry the married character over the barrier.

I am no longer comfortable in the bus. Although I shift and press myself into position on position, no positions satisfy. I feel that I may have dismissed Milo prematurely. I go over the things that I don't want to talk about when Milo comes back. He will want to talk about my abandoned commitments with the theater. He will ask if I am really on my meds. He will wonder what has happened in my mentorship capacity with Zozotte. I will claim ignorance, and he will press in on me with some sort of suffocating interpersonal logic theory, attempting to make me guilty and crestfallen on account of my unpaid debts and my emotional impermeability. He will ignore the topic of my brother, saving it for last so as to blindside me when I'm tired and weak. His loss. I do not tire out. For so long I've been pressing toward true emotion that the other concerns have been passed over.

I get up and walk back to the back of the bus where the wardrobe is and put on a black turtleneck. I stuff a black hat and gloves into the waistband of my pants and proceed out the door and down the steps and onto the gravel parking lot. The crew has packed up and left, except for the youngster, who's leaning against a van smoking a vaporizer.

Blathner is milling about with his hands in his pockets, a Bartles and Jaymes on the ground beside him.

Let's get to the set, he says.

I shrug.

As we walk to the exploded Sebring, he raises his eyebrows at me and I shrug back. That's it? I ask.

Yep, he says. They got what they needed. Plus, the guild wouldn't give them approval to stay longer. Foster's in Los Feliz, inhaling footage.

We get in the car.

Let me give you some advice, he says.

Don't I know it all already?

He pounds my shoulder.

He powers on the car and backs out looking over me over his shoulder. Courage is when you do the right thing at the wrong time, he says.

We spit gravel, tearing out of the parking lot. He continues. The right thing is the thing that gives you strength. Strength is the overcoming of your natural resistances.

We make it onto the highway. Resistances keep you from your passion, he says. Passion is always the wrong thing. Passion is when you could be doing other things.

This is terrible advice.

He guides the car with his left hand. Actually, lemme tell you a story.

I say nothing.

I think it was in 1995 or 1996, and there was this hot-as-shit actor named Alen Gypsum. You ever met him?

No.

Figures, he says. See, he was this golden-haired Midwesterner who was able to adopt the Hollywood accent readily. I was managing him as he came up through the TV commercial and Shakespearean actor racket we had going in those days. His best features were his oversized hands and his golden hair, and he used to wear his shirts open at the neck so his pointy man chest could poke forward out of his shirt. Delish. His gift was to nail every single audition he would get. The actual back end, not so much, but give him an audition and he'd nail it. Get him in the room with a casting director and it was, don't even think about it. The only problem is he thought it was really important to be at each and every single Hollywood party possible. He was so into those parties and the coke was so flowing like the Santa Anas, we all called him Golden Blow.

Right, I say.

So Golden Blow never slept. Instead, he'd get home from a night out and all he had to do to go to work that day was to powder his nose. Long-short, Golden Blow attended so many parties that he was able to find out where the casting crew had their own secret-secret off-Hollywood parties. These parties really weren't any better than regular parties. In fact, they were a bit more subdued and the Fuzz was almost never gonna show up, but they were so subdued that people could talk and network. It wasn't all about banging it out on the dance floor, or playing see-who-can-balance-the-best-handstand-on-the-cornice-side-of-a-ten-story-building, or whatever. So, what we had to do at my agency was to keep this guy from over extending himself. To do this we had to cast big strong guys to go out at night and keep Golden Blow from attending the casting parties. These guys came to our agency to get acting parts, but under the pretense of acting we hired them to go out and act like security at any venue that was hosting one of these off-off casting crew parties. So all these guys began stonewalling Golden Blow, and Golden Blow thought all he had to do was go over their heads so that he could get into these parties. And he was so hopped up on all the roles he got and the coke he blew that he wasn't able to keep track of all the places he'd auditioned at. He wasn't keeping track and we couldn't keep up with him to keep track of him either. So, what happened is that he got so good at auditioning that he found a party planning for a cast of people, I won't call them actors, who would go after him and keep him out of a casting party. And he auditioned for the role, got it, and then saw some producers at another party and got them to help bankroll it. And he ended up shooting this movie about him getting cast in his own movie about stopping himself from being cast in a movie. Man, that film sucked. Straight to video. But on the strength of that story, the movie eventually had a cult following. Anyways, all of his checks are in a filing cabinet in my office in Encino, piling up like Warhols in the seventies. I guess I say all that because I don't want you to be like Alen Gypsum. Don't be that guy. Always cash your checks.

That's it? I ask. That's the moral?

A.B.C.C.—Always Be Cashing—Checks.

I shift back to my side of the car. Any more Philip Glass?

I'll look. How many movies do you think you have in you? he asks.

As many as you want.

Hilarious, he says. You strike me as a person who would never imagine himself to be a sellout.

You can't sell out if you never set a price.

I have so many ideas, the entire possibility of selling out will never be an issue for me.

He turns the wheel. Prove it. I'll make a plan.

I can't, I say. I can't think right now.

Milo has stirred up all kinds of ill will. I tell Blathner that I have to go in search of my brother, my brother the black sheep, the lost child, the child lost in the abyss, the babylike grown man. Or maybe not. Actually, I will hide.

You can dig deep for him in your mind and in your acting, he says, but you're staying with me, and doing this commercial, and finishing this film. The only thing we're searching for here is a paycheck.

I have a question for you, I say.

Shoot.

At the airport, I met the Producer. I wonder, how is he in the position that he's in?

Who cares?

I want to know. It informs my part, I say.

He was a low-level Broadway dweeb, Blathner says. Could never make it at the big show. Inherited all his dough. But that was a long time ago. Made action movies for years. Now he's getting into indies.

Why the prop envelope?

What do you mean?

He gave me an envelope, I say. It was empty. I opened it. He told me to open it and nothing was inside.

Don't overthink it.

I have nothing to go on except what happens with these people acting in the film. The Producer gave me an empty envelope. I assume he means not to pay me.

It wasn't a prop, he says. He must've forgot to put the Dodgers tickets in it.

Always Be Cashing Checks, eh? What if the person giving out the checks won't give them anymore?

Dunno, he says. There's the union and the guild. These producers don't really have that much latitude. I rammed your contract through, and it was all speed checked. I made sure they used my boilerplate. I double checked the double checks. We're in no danger.

But what does it mean?

When Blathner talks, I squirm. But his presence is reassuring. And nothing rattles him. I long to bury myself under his breast. There is no other agent-slash-manager for me. He is out and out for all to see. Sure, some agents claim to be about high art—that is all just lies. An agent should be an agent, the actor should worry about the glossolalia. Banality has its place.

We make good time for a while, and I talk to him, and he talks to me, and I talk to myself about what I imagine I will do when we arrive at the commercial. The light of the morning threatens, and we will arrive through morning rush hour at a time that is appropriate for this shoot. I am already dressed, so it will be quick and neat, and I will not have to overthink it.

He parks the car in a quiet neighborhood, gets out and points at the house I will rob. I begin to sit low in the seat and stretch my legs, resisting the floor. He walks toward the mobile production trailers and enters one. Any noise annoys an oyster, but a noisy noise annoys an oyster most. I wait the prescribed ten minutes.

I am running from a car. I am running in a yard. A car, a yard, a fence. I hop and manage to keep off kilter. I like the lighting. The lighting is the best thing about this shoot. I make the window ajar. Up and over, I penetrate the room. I see jewelry. The room is well lit too. The sheets are asunder. I pass over the jewelry. I undress the bed. I caress the sheets. The sheets are in my hands and I am swaddling myself in their softness. They smell like plastic. I connect with their plasticity and present my face around the room with the mechanical chops I imagine a commercial actor finds necessary in order to move merch. I roll the sheets into a ball like a pompom. I throw them out the window and follow. I am heaving, lugging loose sheets, running over a grassy yard. There is Blathner. Blathner closes his flip phone and gets in the car initiating the engine. As I fumble with the sheet and the car door, a small person in tight-fitting ashen clothing wearing a shoulder bag approaches me from where I do not know and in a swift motion reaches out with squat utility shears and snips a measure of the sheet, squirreling it away in a bag. Without thinking much, I capture a wrist and it feels slender, but I do not see the face. But I can tell it is a girl.

Release, she says.

Take the entire sheet, I say.

She wrenches her wrist free and escapes and I stand watching her disappear into the neighborhood. I am tangled up in the sheet. She is gone.

I ponder.

I get into the Sebring. Blathner engages reverse and gets the commercial people on the phone.

We good? he asks.

We good? I ask.

We good, he says.

How do I like my apples? Yellow. How do I like my skin? Moist. How do I like my therapists? Unpaid. There remains the question of Milo. What will he do? There remains the question of Oliver's performance of my old role at the theater. Will he fail? There remains Zozotte's plight. Will she work and develop, or will she waste her talent? In addition to this there remains a film to be made. Above all of it is, what is going on with my brother? I stare at the hole in my sheet.

Blathner wants none of this. As we drive, we are in it for the it of it. Rush hour is upon us and my mind is a fever of hapless noise. I put the seat all the way up so that my back is beyond straight. I press my head forward so that it is near the glass. I press up with my hands on the seat and force my legs and thighs to contract so that the force of my arms and the stretching of my body can get into my muscles. The sheet is permanently wrecked.

We continue on and on. I get in a significant leg workout. I decline the offer of a cigarette. My back is a sprung coil. Blathner has decided that he will smoke a cigarette with the windows rolled up, and so I smoke by association with the windows rolled up. The Bartles and Jaymes are drank. I am working on my arms, next my palms, next my neck.

Give me the gift of a grip-top sock, a dip-drape shipshape tip-top sock, not your spiv-slick slapstick slip-slop stock, but a plastic, elastic, grip-top sock. None of your fantastic slack-swap stock from a slapdash flash-cash haberdasher shop; not a knick-knack knock-kneed knickerbocker sock with a mock-shot blob-mottled trick-ticker clock; not a rucked up, puckered up, flop-top sock, nor a super-sheer seersucker rucksack sock, not a spot-speckled frog-freckled cheap sheik's sock off a hodgepodge moss-blotched scotch-botched block; nothing slip-shop, drip-drop, flip-flop, or glip-glop; tip me to a tip-top grip-top sock.

Promoting the film is the best career move I can think of, Blathner says.

Yes, I say. And to promote the film in a way that would work and a way that would matter. I see in my mind's eye an emergent flash. It must not be ersatz, I say. I will not go on talk shows. And no podcasts. I will, however, write poems for *The New Yorker*. I will, however, ride a hot air balloon with Lucia over a swamp of alligators. I think about the footage of the train passing over me. It is a perfect picture of the tenor of this piece.

I tell Blathner that the footage of me going under the train should be cobbled into a makeshift shaky handheld short film of how the film has gone awry.

He shrugs then yells, Are you serious? at the absolutely stopped traffic on the 405. Contrived, he says to me. Early millennial stuff.

A picture forms. I get a vision of a spectacular costume with a billboard on the back. I describe for him a skintight suit of dark fabric with tubes of fluorescent lighting up the legs and down the arms and up my spine onto the top of my head. It has glow tape up and down it and glowing hashes on my hands, feet, and face.

Where would you wear this? He asks.

I tell him I'm getting to it. And then, I say we will build an enormous marquee on my back. It will say *TONE POEM*. In that way, I'll stump for the film.

Although that fits you perfectly, Blathner says, it sounds like something that would only work for one day. He puts a Steve Reich CD into the deck of his dash. He continues, It would have to be done as some kind of spectacle. It would need to grab the attention of masses of people all at once. You can't just traipse around a city street. Not big enough. It's got to be bigger than all that. In other words, the suit is just the message. What about the venue?

Let's make the suit and think of that later, I say.

As we chitchat and drive, we talk about what it takes for a film to excel. He claims peace is what ruins every potential film. He says peace is for the weak. He insists that what makes films fail is that they are shackled by their flowers. They are insulated. They are a kind of failed church, one too removed from the world to be of any good.

The argument is convincing, but his views are too cynical. Yes, acting, art, beauty should be violent. But he is arguing more for an action movie than for a gesture that breaks into the cold composure of an audience member. Can I even say audience member and maintain my integrity as a proponent of the theater of cruelty? Instead, the audience must be integrated, assimilated, subsumed by the verity of the tableau. No bystander should be let out of the range of the violence of this kind of stagecraft. Blathner wants cheap explosions and ruddy heroes carting weak bathos-laden victims to safety. My work is to flip all of that on its head. To plunge any scene in any place into an uncompromising crucible.

He flips his blinker on to change lanes. It clicks twice. He changes lanes.

I am well-stretched and tender as we turn into the driveway of the production compound in Los Feliz. Nothing has changed with the set. There is a hodgepodge of crew members acting busy, moving truck from here to there. I step out of the car and Blathner puts up his fist as if I will knock it, and he says he can't wait to get home and sleep. He suggests the same for me, but I remain skeptical it will do me any good.

He speeds away.

A crew member nods and congratulates me on last night's shoot. Claims it was a fine piece of work. There is much more to do, I say. I ask him what he did. He starts to talk about—

I continue on and then enter the house off to the side and Avril is there in my dressing room, sitting casually with one leg over the armrest of a chair. She wears high-top sneakers, and a skirt over pants, and a tight tank top, and bangles.

Reading? I ask.

My lines for the play, she says.

That old thing? I counter. Brunch?

She shuts the playbook.

We leave the room and turn out into the middle of the compound toward the catering truck.

You look violent, she says.

We get to the roach coach thing. I want tofu, seaweed, marinated eel, brown rice.

She wants a salad niçoise.

On a whim, I also order a Monte Cristo. We both add on a French Press and a bottle of Gerolsteiner.

They have everything here, she says.

They?

We take a picnic table under an umbrella and she relays a bit about how she cannot break into Oliver's solitary mind space. I ask about the Brute.

The Brute is pining, she says. We're all pretty uptight about the play. And Oliver, she says, don't forget Oliver. You gotta talk to him. He seems unstable. He sleepwalked into this role. He doesn't seem to have his wits about him. Not sure how he'll pull it off.

I say, I will. But where is he?

Don't know, she says.

The French press arrives. I see from the corner of my eye a PA approaching stealthily. We are given knives and forks and chopsticks. I sit on the table's top so I can survey the area. I cradle my rice bowl in my left hand, protecting it from the prospect of the approaching PA absconder, and I individually pincer rice grains, lifting them to my mouth in fluid but exaggerated gestures. It feels right to concentrate on each bite the way a hungry person would, if that person had all the time in the world to nitpick. The problem with rice is, though, I say, you have to take a lot of it all at once for it to make any substantive difference. There is no taste in a single grain. It is not powerful enough to do anything individually.

The PA gathers up enough nerve to stand next to us.

Avril asks her if she can help her.

The PA says no, but that there's a meeting with Foster, like, right away, and can she help us?

You know Oliver? I ask.

She looks like she doesn't, but acts like she does. Sure.

We need to speak with him, Avril says.

The PA flees toward the other PAs.

I start to eat. I really do.

The rice is gone, and, drinking the Gerolsteiner, I slather the eel with wasabi. It is gone. I wrap up the tofu in the seaweed, and it is gone. It is time to plunge The Press. We pour out cups of the stuff in our paper cups left over from the Gerolsteiner. I don't even feel close to feeling full, but I do feel my mortality. It is serious eating.

Avril reflects on the fear Oliver has curried in all of the performers. He brings his camera to rehearsal, she says. The Impresario indulges him. He's playing the part as a camera-clad neurotic, she says. And yet, that's who he is. But no one thinks he can pull it off. He's unstable.

What are your exchanges with him like? I ask between bites of the luxurious egg-drenched brioche and slurps of coffee.

He's like a bop bag, she says. A pushover who always bounces back. He takes a line like it's a heavy punch, but then comes back at me with a kind of passive aggressive force. Like he's permanently wired, but also interminably given to failure. And he's preternaturally resilient. Then he goes off on his own just when the conflict begins to seem real.

The PAs leave their table, and all disappear together as a group.

Gravitas, I say.

Barren beacon beckons bacon baron, she says.

Round the rugged rocks the ragged rascals ran.

She nods. Toy boat, toy boat, toy boat.

With her salad halfly finished and my body bloated, I want to be alone. I don't want a cigarette, and I wonder if Oliver is even in the compound.

He's not here, I say.

No shit, she says.

I am nauseous. Maybe I should smoke.

I excuse myself and run toward a planter, near a wall, next to a power generator. I make sick.

Avril's standing over me with a napkin. Foster's running you through the ringer, Avril says. In a good way. The voices, the allusions. Your control, your plastic repertoire. Everything's present that needs to be—gesture, heroism, humility. You look unconscious.

I continue to make sick. The PAs have kept everyone back from me. A certain kind of person, I say, can understand the explanation of a joke, but cannot laugh. They hear sounds, but not music. They do not comprehend us.

It's great work, Avril says.

As I turn, I see that something does not look right. One of the PAs remains. She appears too wise, dodgy. I stumble toward her. She turns her back to me. She grasps something in her hand. Her face is permanently set in my mind. My stomach is empty, and I must hydrate. I tell Avril to watch the PA—the one with the army boots and the pink bow in her hair. Don't let her out of your sight, I whisper. I leave for the dressing room.

The hand of nothing condescends for me to grasp—such that I overlook my own industry, my own artistry, my own self. I am in need of saving. I am reassured by the possibility that I am a horrible person—that I am never acting—that who I play and who I am are completely conceived in deception and pain. The two are the same, and I am not able to save myself from it. I need the audience just like they need me to show them their inadequacy.

I struggle, and I always struggle with moving from scene to scene without adequate development. There are so many factors in any one scene, it is a wonder if anyone can put even one single good scene or setting into any performance. I struggle to adequately develop the look, tension, smell, environment, dialogue, internal thoughts, infernal thoughts—everything swirling around in any one particular place at any one time. Almost certainly, I do too much and think too much simultaneously. Two dimensions, three dimensions, too much to play. Instead, a single solitary interaction needs to occur, a believable fiction, enough singularity so that I am believed, and the disbelief is believed.

In the dressing room, I rip off my clothes, and take a bottle of water and a toothbrush, and clean out my mouth. I pour myself a bowl of broth, and take it with me into the shower. It is something comforting to drink warm broth while showering in hot water.

I leave the shower and towel off. The room is lit in a kind of harsh light that only makes sense in the context of all the leafy potted plants. It is all like an Henri Rousseau.

I wonder what I should wear to meet with Foster. It seems I haven't spoken with him in days. I find a tight, drab, striped shirt. I throw on a dark tie over that. There are some black velvet pants that look good over purple patent leather oxfords. White socks. Patent belt. I find some pomade and work it into my hair slowly. I drink another bowl of broth, no spoon, urinate, and exit the room with a camel hair cardigan over my shoulder.

Outside, the crew has set up a prohibitively obfuscated approach to Foster's trailer. Exactly. What else am I here for?

I try to make it as simple as possible. I stroll. I make myself aware of the environment so that each step is a solid one, deliberate, distinct, and profound. Then I rush. The walk just seems to call for that.

I knock on Foster's trailer door.

Come in, I hear.

I stand fussy and wait.

Come in, Foster says louder.

I wait impatiently.

Lucia opens the door. Where have you been?

The lighting is poor. Lucia wears an all-black suit, hair pulled taut behind her head. Shiny black stilettos. Sport coat. White hoops for earrings. It makes her well-seasoned skin glow, even in this light.

Foster sits between us. He has one earbud stuck in his ear. A boom mic drops down from the ceiling. He wears a white V-neck shirt and striped trousers. A scarf of course.

This is about your brother Boniface, he says.

We call him B.F., I say.

I threw him off the set this morning—he was prowling around—looking for you—said you invited him—what do you want me to do?

He looked distraught, Lucia says.

I want to speak with him, I say. But the time is not right just now. I think it is good for me, what he is doing, bringing problems to my work.

That's so hypocritical, Lucia says. She is clenching her cheeks, and the lines form down her nose, indicating that B.F. has taken her in. Somehow, he has worked quickly and deftly to turn Lucia against me.

Have you slept with him? I ask.

When I say this, Foster is taken aback like he has found some sort of treasure. Then his eyes roll back in his head, and it seems that he is listening to something in his earbud.

You're mad, Lucia says. Then laughs.

Did you want to? I return.

He's a nobody, she says. What have I to do with him?

The feeling in the trailer is rich. I am looking forward to what Foster will say. Do you want him on the set? I ask.

Yes, and for the sake of the film, he says. Then he says, I have to ask you a series of questions—and please note that your timing here is extremely important for obvious reasons—consistency, integrity, comprehensiveness of scope—I'm only going to ask these questions once.

K.

On a scale of one to ten, one being not at all, ten being absolutely, answer the following questions as you can.

. . .

Question. Do you feel that your bulimia is getting in the way of your work?

One.

Do you want to harm others?

Ten.

Are you sleeping daily?

One.

Do you have someone with whom you can confide?

Ten.

Do you want to harm yourself?

Ten.

Do you feel you have practical life skills to get you from day to day with a reasonable measure of effectiveness?

Ten.

Do you feel safe in this place?

One.

Are you hearing voices?

Ten.

Wow, okay, wow—let's switch gears a bit.

K.

Multiple choice—You are in a forest—A tree is about to fall—It leans dangerously—You decide to push it over—Choose one of the following: A), Do you push it over to ensure the forest is safe for others?—Do you B), push it over for the sheer enjoyment of watching it fall?—Or, do you C), regret pushing it over?

B, I say. I push it over for the sheer pleasure of watching it fall. I am a poet.

Lucia laughs in a stifled way, in mockery.

Question: What is the school of poetry that you most align yourself with?

Clairvoyance.

Yes—Alright—Question. A kitten is in a guillotine—Your brother is in a guillotine—You only have time to run to one of the two guillotines to stay the blade—Which of the helpless victims do you save?

Neither, I say. The entity placing them in that situation is responsible. I just happen to be passing through.

Thank you, Foster says.

My turn, I say.

Shoot.

May we have the night off to go to Avril's play? I ask.

We?

Me and Lucia.

Yes but, Foster says, after we shoot the flophouse scene.

Of course, I say.

Lucia's voice takes on a bitter tambour. I'd love to see the play, she says. Just not with you.

Foster breathes out of his nose in desperation. Milo wants to talk to you, Foster says. He peels off one of his earbuds and offers it to me. I put it in my ear, but to do so, I lean in to Foster. Our faces are right up close to each other. I am staring full on in the face of Foster. He does not blink. He does not look away.

Godot? Milo says.

Yes? I say, orienting myself. Where's the mic?

The room's the mic, Foster says.

His face has a latency to it. It seeks to drain whatever it encounters. His apparently unkempt stubble is perfectly groomed, so that any outliers have been cut close to the skin. He also appears to have recently tweezed his eyebrows.

Don't let your brother in, bro, Milo says. Maybe somewhere down the line, but not now. You'll cave.

I will take this into consideration, I say.

Passivity, brah, plays into everyone's psychosomatic development. By that I mean chillax.

I focus my eyes on Foster's and decide not to blink. He does not blink either. We do not blink. He is the ever-probing eye of independent film.

Milo asks me what I'll do about my bro, brah. Milo tells me my brother is not welcome on the set.

We will have to do the shoot off set then, I say.

Milo gasps.

That's it, I say.

Brah?

So that's it? Foster says.

The Brute has the lines? I ask.

Foster blinks. Isn't Brutus in the play?

I disengage. I text the Brute to see where he is. The way he sausage-fingers his phone, any intelligible response will do.

He texts, I think, the affirmative, and that I'm lucky he's round about. He'll meet me at an Uber in front of the production compound.

I turn to Lucia. You ready?

I'll take a separate car.

Foster approves, giving the gesture for a certain degree of completion. Better if we meet you there anyway.

As I leave, Foster is placing his arm around Lucia's shoulders, and she puts one of his earbuds in her ear, and it looks as if they have something really important to tell each other. And I hope so. Lucia's game needs upping for the next scene.

I put on my cashmere cardigan and stroll, hands in pockets, down the trailer steps, and out into the center of the compound. A PA approaches immediately, hands me my eye makeup, and tells me to do it sloppily. Asks me again if I won't mind letting makeup make me up. Verity, I say. I open the compact. I work toward harsh lines.

We walk toward the front of the compound.

The Brute joins. Hey.

The Brute looks like a cross between an old Brando and an old Nolte. We aim to leave the set. He holds out his phone as if it will attract the car. I have to admit it is a telling gesture. He smiles because the driver arrives right away. He waves with his fingers and he gets in and shuts the door behind him, locking it, and scoots to the far side of the car. I laugh and motion to the driver to unlock the door.

The Brute says no, and he and the driver exchange a few words inside the car before the driver rolls down the passenger window and asks me if I will behave.

I agree to behave.

He tells me that if the Brute feels uncomfortable, I'll have to get out of the car immediately.

I say that I have no control over how Brutus will react, and that maybe Brutus could take his own car. The driver says fine, then rolls up the window, and the Brute has a few words with the driver who looks over at me, then the Brute gets out of the car, and the car drives away without the Brute.

What was all that about? The Brute asks.

You started it, I say.

What do I have to do to get you to cooperate?

If I have to tell you, then you don't know what you're doing.

The Brute punches at his phone. As we wait for another car, I take a seat on the curb, patent leather shoes in the gutter, elbows on my knees. He turns the opposite way to talk at the production compound.

She really wants to make things right, he says.

I want to make things right also.

He wrings his hands and puts them into his back pockets. His phone chirps and he brings it to his face. It's Avril, he says. She saw the PA with the pink hair bow scoop up a sample size serving of your puke and store it away in a little glass jar.

I ask him to ask her to describe the PA.

Suspicious, he says. Dodgy, but fluid. She was only acting as if she were cleaning up the puke.

I nod to myself. I tell him not to tell Avril anything, that it's better to just let things run their course.

Uh-huh, says the Brute. He says bye. He buffets my shoulder.

I turn to give him the look that we've been through battles, that our friendship has been through so much, that I am still willing to go further, and that we have an understanding between the two of us that we will never give up—that he and I will always be friends.

Another car comes. I open the door to duck in, but he slams the door on my body.

You don't love her, he says.

I never said I did, I say.

The driver gets out of the car and looks dumbstruck.

There's no damage to the car, the Brute says, and he turns back toward the compound and walks. See you at the play.

It hurts, but I am not hurt, and I get into the back seat to sit low in the car. The driver stands outside for a while, then gets in.

Here we go, he says.

As the car moves cautiously, I take my phone and turn it on, ignoring all alerts. In the sunset hours, the Los Angeles landscape exudes a kind of mystical regret that compels me to grieve. I've never really felt at home here. I consider myself an immigrant. I touch through my phone to Oliver and call.

One ring.

Hello? Gargon? Hi.

I'm not hearing good things, I say.

All the bad things are true, Oliver says.

I'll be at the play tonight, I say.

Oh, would you? He says. That'd be great.

Great.

What am I doing, you ask? He asks. You wonder?

Pray tell.

Well, I'll tell you. I'm just sitting here casually brooding. I brood because I'm sure that I'm just a placeholder for someone else, and I cannot look to the past or a cultural tradition. I must instead traffic in the spectacle of the banal present. Know anyone like that?

I am not rejoining the cast, I say. Inactivity is depression's best friend. Do it right, I say. Do not put yourself together, pull yourself apart.

What's the use? Oliver says. I brood, he adds. I brood about how people overlook my intelligence, my sensitivity, my talent. But I can't act anyway. And even if I could, I wouldn't do it right. Plus, I have the worst luck anyway. And I'd only get hurt. And, really good acting has never really been done before, or at least I've never known anyone who's ever done it, and it's not what you know anyway. And everyone's gonna laugh, and I should just wait for the right time. I need to better prepare anyway. Now's not my time.

There, there, I say.

What's that?

There.

You're making fun of me!

Where are you? I ask.

I'm at the cemetery, he says. Forest Lawn.

Of course?

I go to cemeteries to take snaps of recent grave markers—ones that people have put in after I was born. And I collect obituaries of people who were born after I was born.

Sounds sensible.

What?

The performance sounds promising. I'm looking forward to the performance.

You'd love seeing me suffer, he says.

No, I heart you, I say. You're a muse. Believe what you have is valuable.

This play is my obituary.

But you're beautiful, I say. A person like you is a person who makes things great no matter how they look.

You mock me sir. You mock me. I'm photographing the phone as we speak.

I laugh and he does not laugh back. I have no other response to give as he is in the very best place to play the role he is in.

I hang up.

The drive proceeds. My phone finds my pocket. A dark cloud descends. Why is it so hard to be straight with oneself? Oliver cannot self-examine without an intermediary.

In a flash, at a gutter on the street I see a thin man digging in the mud with his hands. He unearths a grate. He pulls the grate off its hinges and begins lowering himself into the storm system. I am riveted. Then, he disappears into the underground. What is down there?

The car continues. The driver makes attempts at small talk. Quite a bit of traffic today, he says.

Every day, I say.

The driver strikes me as ex-navy. His hair is short and well-cropped. His body has those knotty muscles, somewhat developed, but sculpted soft by the deprivation of seven months at a time at sea.

This your full-time job? I ask.

Yep, he says. But I'm also a full-time actor.

He does have some charisma. He talks out the side of his face with his chin up, and kind of throws his words back at me in an attempt to connect directly, that style of drive and talk that works so well. He's wearing an oatmeal henley.

What do you think about peace? I ask. Because I think peace is for the weak.

I'm thinking my answer will affect my tip, he says. He says it gruff.

Hey, this is chit-chat. I'm not out to get you.

He puts his head back on the headrest. I think peace has made us all soft, he says. People don't even know what hardship is about.

We're all weak, so we want peace.

And peace is good, but for the weak? He shakes his head and laughs to himself.

I grab the back of his seat and push my head into the front of the car. We are all weak in some way.

He tenses up.

And are we finally ready to give peace a chance? I ask. It really is the only defensible policy orientation.

He looks like he forces himself not to react.

We ride in silence for a while. I look at my phone, look at the window, put my phone away again, take my phone out, roll down the window a bit, edge my phone out the window and drop it onto the street. It bangs against the car as it drops.

What was that? He says.

A phone, I say. I don't want anyone to know where I'm at.

I guess the ride's over? He asks. Even though we're almost there, he adds.

No, the ride's not on my phone, I say. My friend will pay for it. I'll tell him to tip high.

That would be nice, he says.

I get his attention and hand him two twenties anyway—just to be on the safe side, I say. Then I ask what kind of actor he is.

A stand in, he says. People tell me I have an extremely active back of the head. He laughs again.

You're cast well. Composure is important.

But, I want to get in front of the camera. I'm working on my pathos.

How does one work on one's pathos? I ask.

That's the thing, he says. I think it's about making friends. What's more heartbreaking than going after new people and being ready for them, and changing your life for them, only to find out they think very little of you?

I have friends like that, I say. I aim to love those people anyway. But I see your point.

He rolls the steering wheel. I think a really great way to develop pathos is to be friends with someone who doesn't want anything to do with you.

Makes sense, I say. Like what an actor's always trying to do with an audience.

Usually, it's with family.

True, I say. So true. Anyways, what's your name?

Steve, he says. Yours?

Godot.

Like Beckett?

My father had a certain affinity for the literary.

I've always wanted to be an author, he says.

Certainly.

Steve pulls up to the curb and puts the car into park.

Would you drop me off around the block? I say. I want to work on my approach.

O-kay.

I flatten my hair and wipe the excess pomade on the seats of the car. I hope you get the kind of role you really want, I say. And that you never run out of work. And that you're willing to get violent enough to find peace.

I hope so too, Steve says.

I hope so too—as well.

Fare well, he says.

Good pun, Steve.

I get out of the car and give him one thumb up and a half wave, and I plunge my hands into the pockets of my pants. I put my shoulders up toward my head and try to make myself taller. Six sticky skeletons. Six sticky skeletons. Six sticky skeletons.

This neighborhood is sad. The heat is oppressive. A plastic bag blows by. There are dead weeds rising up from cracks in the sidewalks. And this is a block away from the Sunset Strip.

I see the rundown apartments we are to shoot at. There are some lights on in the windows, but nothing extraordinarily bright. I begin to walk. I step on and off and get into a rhythm. I step on a crack. I build up speed and the force of a tumbling presence pulls me forward. And yet, I sense something behind me.

I make it to the door. I hit the intercom buzzer.

What do you want? It says.

I'm here for the party, I say.

Party of one, it says.

The door buzzes, and I grip the handle and the door frame and pull myself in. There's a flight of wood stairs leading up and twisting around from flight to flight. I pull myself up by the railing. This place is squalid. The floors are missing tiles. There are flies. Single light bulbs brighten whole hallways, which are suffocatingly small. My footsteps echo as I approach the door. I knock. I wait. I stand again and knock again. It is quiet behind the door.

I move myself up to the front of the door so that I'm standing in the door jamb, so that when the door opens, I can lean into the apartment.

A bolt unlatches and dangles, scraping against the inside of the door. A tumbler rolls over in its housing and as the door opens, I jam my foot into the crack and yell, Hello. The acrid scent of incense hits me, and it is hot like an oven, and the smoke billows out into the hall. An angular guy with a huge unshaven Adam's apple and an unwashed mullet asks, Hello?

Party of one.

Oh, it's you, he says. Sorry man. Want a Mickey's?

Like, a full Mickey's? I ask.

What, you have to leave already?

We walk to the kitchen, which is strewn with boxes and trash and a garden gnome, and he opens the fridge and gives me a 40 oz Mickey's. It's cold and full of potential, and I can't say I'm not intrigued.

It's on me, he says.

I hit him on the back. You're in that Toy World band? I ask.

Yeah. I'm Bram.

I've seen you guys before. You're the dancer. Quite dubious. You played a while back at that noise show in East Hollywood. You stunk. But you know, in a good way.

We bang Mickey's.

I take a drink. It is uncompromisingly bad, and I ham up a reaction to the excruciatingly acerbic taste.

Bram is amused.

I can hear exchanges of conversation around the corner in the living room. Someone's riffing calliope. The apartment is squalid and tiny, and the cameras and lighting are well-hidden in the ceilings and the walls. There is a group of people fronting a lit fireplace, drinking and talking in the living room, and as I walk on the creaking floor, I can hear Lucia's voice from behind a door in the hall. I try the door and it is locked.

Bram shakes his head, like as if to say don't even try it. I hear the mumbled voice of a man behind the door, but the words sound unconscionable.

Lucia, I say to the door.

Yeah? What?

It's me.

I begin to play the scene in a half-despondent way, giving weight to the alcohol and favoring alternate high and low registration in my voice. She is not happy to hear me; she will not open the door. The man inside makes no noise.

Who's in there, I ask, putting the emphasis on the who's.

What are you doing here? she says.

Fuck this, Bram says, tipping his 40 back and walking around the corner toward the living room.

I put the Mickey's down on the floor and lean my face against the door with my arms up just to feel the resonance of the scene.

I can feel you through the door, I say.

Go away.

I want you to open up of your own will, I say. I want you to want to do it.

I can't, she says. For your sake. I won't.

With my face up against the door, I sense that there is something going on here that is more sinister than simply what I can sense.

Who is it in there with you? I ask.

Silence.

Hey Guy, I say.

He doesn't respond. There is no movement behind the door.

I'm telling you, Lucia says. It's better if you don't know.

The deep sense of dread begins to seep into me through the door, through where my cheek is touching the door, and it begins to dawn on me who it is. My brother has taken up with Lucia. Foster has made this all come about—orchestrated it very well.

To approach my brother, I must reach out my hand in fear to shake my own hand—the handle—and it must turn.

I put my hand out. What about the play? I think about how to approach. Everything that once had round edges is square.

To my shock the door handle turns in my hand. It is unlocked.

I enter and Lucia scowls. She is wearing a negligee. She neglects to cover herself with her open bath robe. In a chair on the far side of the room there is the form of a man sitting in a chair. He wears a sheet draped over his head so his face is hidden.

Here's your chance, Lucia says.

Chance to what? I say. Accept his apology?

The reverse, she says. Do it. Put an end to all of this.

In the poor lighting, there is only a spattering of light caressing the sitting form and all else is dark. I reach out my hand. Is it you? I ask.

The form nods, but still there is no speech.

I begin to realize I've been had. I reach forward and tear the sheet off. It takes a second for the shock to register, and I sit still for a second before it does. It is Milo.

Hey brah.

It is just like my brother to be absent for his own apology. It is just like Foster to stall and punch up the tension for the climax. Here comes the gut punch.

You're not ready for your brother, Lucia says.

It's true, Milo says. He puts the sheet back over his head. Brah. It's not avant-garde to run away from a play when there's still so much left to learn. And it's not avant-garde to run away from your bro when you have the sweet option of reconciliation.

The shadows and lighting shift and arrange themselves in various color profiles like they are set up on a disco ball. I sit myself down and shift in multiple postures on a velour camelback sofa. Then I get up to leave.

No, wait, Lucia says. I have something to say.

What is it?

I've never spoken with your brother.

She pulls her robe tight around herself and gestures toward Milo, who cannot even see her. From what I've heard, she says, your brother's not clever, he's smart. He's not a deep thinker, he's driven. He doesn't care about people, but he's kind. And he's not a loser.

You're saying that to wound me, I say.

And he has a fondness for puppets, she finishes.

I turn around and close the door behind me. I pick up my Mickey's and walk into the living room. There is a group of people sitting around playing the board game Candyland, and Bram stands against the wall. They're burning some aromatic mugwort to help with the smell and the breathing. A hairy guy in a vest plays the calliope, and I nod at him while he gingerly snails around on the keys. I'm Insalubre, I say. A long-haired guy with a pink face in a three-piece suit says he's Harrod. There's a tidily dressed man wearing creased slacks and a tight Polo sweater sitting cross-legged. He nods. Next to him is a sixty-ish year-old woman wearing beads and a dashiki. She's knitting. Wanna play? she asks.

Candyland? I say with disdain.

Or not, she says.

Time stands still in this place. Harrod takes a card. He's winning, nearest to the finish line, but the card he pulls is a gum drop card and he has to move himself back near the beginning of the board. He's happy about this. It appears that this group of people does this all day all the time.

Why's that good? I ask.

The woman looks up from knitting. Best to spend as much time in the candy as possible.

Yeah, Bram agrees. Who wants to finish when you can just stay in the candy forever?

The tidily dressed man says linear is dead.

I look over at Bram. Lucia and Milo appear in the hall. Milo is still wearing the sheet.

Whasup, Milo says.

The group says hello to Milo in unison.

Lucia and Milo stand near the game. The calliope music picks up in rhythm. Everyone begins to get up one at a time to dance. The music is not unenchanting. The knitter wraps a belt of macramé around my shoulders and pulls me in to dance, and I start to shuffle step, then we dance lightly, then just kind of sway gently, and then the group joins us and we sway reprehensibly, and we all dance for a while, but all in all it all feels wrong. It feels I am sucked into a vortex, a hive mind, a solipsism. The pace picks up, and we move from a sway to a shuffle. We're treading on the Candyland board and the pieces are being cast about the room until the music begins again to slow and the vibe drains out of the room and every possible visual and angle has been captured and registered.

When I begin to bore, I nod to Bram. The play, I say to Lucia.

I duck out into the hall, then out of the apartment and down the stairs, and out into the street in the dull pain of approaching evening. Lucia follows, struggling to get a pair of pointe shoes on and tied, and she wears her negligee and a tight-cut coat over the top. She joins me.

I nod.

She puts her hand on my shoulder to hold herself up and tie off her shoes. They've set up the dolly tracks right over there, she says.

I see it. Foster has rails set up down the street so the camera can roll and shoot. And there is a crew prepping.

She dusts her cheeks with a brush, then chucks it into the gutter.

We walk.

When we get next to the camera I can see where our mark is. Rear weird real wheels, real weird rear wheels, wired rear real wheels. We hit the mark, and she starts.

I have no opinion about your brother, she says. I just want us to be happy.

Insalubre comes forward. Since I don't know what to do about it, I write about it, Insalubre says. It becomes tangible, and I can think about it. Then I can show it to someone else, and they can read about it. Then it frees me up to forget about it. And then, so now, that's all I can say about it.

She sends me a staggered look.

Talk isn't helping, I say.

Then what are we doing? She asks.

I stop her and stand in front of her, my hands on her shoulders. I close up her coat, and she shrugs, and we play it up with gesture and attention, mugging. Her sadness is with me and with a look of uncompromising careful deliberation. Then I turn her around and place my hands in her hands and then our hands trail off as I turn and begin to run and the camera on the track follows me down the sidewalk for one continuous shot of the remainder of the block. Then I stop and turn and shout, Farewell.

She puts out her hand to wave as the crew down near her side of the block captures the reverse shot, and I wave back and then run again, continue to run down the street until I am off on my own.

The intensity of walking in end-of-day Los Angeles should debilitate, but instead it complicates. The cars that clog the roadway are classic, in some way, in the slanting light. At any moment, I expect to be harried and bowled over, but instead they insist me on, and they floor it, then come to a stop, and I can continue on.

I think of my brother. I am no longer the person I was one hour ago. I cannot think without thinking of him. He is responsible for every bit of energy I have dedicated to going on and on. He is a one-man unpredictable freeform acting seminar. He is a Colossus of Rhodes. It is why I must stay away from him.

I continue on toward the theatre, and it is no short walk. I luxuriate in the time. I walk on and that is just fine as the temperature wells up from within me.

I continue on. I arrive.

I enter the back of the theatre and see Avril. She's gesturing and moving well in her own energy veil. She wears black shorts, jellies, and a tube top. Flip-flops. Nauseating. She sees me and tells me Zozotte is talking about me.

I can smell the smell of vomit. Some actor, somewhere, is absent-mindedly noodling on a zither. These back-of-house rooms are disorienting. There is an offensive mix of high-pitched screeching and then crescendos of anger. Rhony and Zozotte are talking. She tells him what the Impresario says, about the art critic Guy Brett, that it's about the emphasis on the group, not the individual. That it's about work produced in conditions of great insecurity. That, due to urgency, it's about craft employing only the materials close at hand. Rhony wears a fluorescent windbreaker and a floppy knitted hat. Zozotte has a wooly scarf tied around her neck and a short black skirt and black translucent leggings. She's leaning against the wall, pointing the toe of her shoe. Rhony's got a shopping bag, and his hat rides precariously on his fro. He's kind of swaying a bit, and I have no frame of reference.

I see Oliver. I motion over to him. He stands there for a bit, lost in thought, and then he confirms that I am motioning over to him, and he takes his camera and starts taking photos. Rhony and Zozotte laugh at each other. Help me! Oliver says. How can I push past the limits I've placed on myself? When do I know when I've pushed too far? Can I push too far? How would I know?

It is something to see what Oliver sees. Going through the motions of snapping shots bears fruit. Rhony panders for the camera, then decides to tickle Zozotte, then falls to the floor laughing with her. Oliver gets up on a chair and shoots downward. In all of this Avril and Zozotte's shoes are in all the shots. Flip-flops and Nikes. Oliver is elated.

Describe impending doom, I say. Depict the gradual darkening of the horizon as the points of view stack up. Show us the suffocating cloud.

Sneak the camera in, Zozotte says. Put it under your shirt, then whip it out on stage when it's too late.

I nod to Zozotte, but she avoids my look, then looks back and keeps her attention on Oliver. Avril, shaking her head walks out of the room.

Go find your seat, Zozotte says to me.

What is it that is keeping us apart? I ask.

I can't tell when you're joking and when you're being serious, she says.

I don't joke to make light of things.

What are you wearing? She asks.

I'm flirting with my darker side, I say. I find that a complete revision in appearance goes a long way toward seeing each movement of life with new eyes.

I gotta go finish a project, Rhony says.

Bye-bye.

Have you spoken with your brother? Zozotte asks.

My brother hasn't shown his face.

He's everywhere, she says. He was on set looking for you. I don't know why you can't work something out with him. Don't you think that's important? What kind of person can't make up with his brother?

It's not that simple, I say.

She shakes her head.

Is that so hard to believe?

Your brother is amazing. I have kind of a social media crush on him, she tells me.

Like a clown.

You should see the things he posts. She puts her phone in front of me.

My brother has his own YouTube channel, apparently. There are videos of him showering. Him hitting parked cars when riding on his bike. He slaps strangers and runs away. He accomplishes record runs on tactical weapons courses with semi-automatic assault weapons and finishes with a knife slash to the neck of a stationary dummy saying, Take that intifada! He wears a Speedo seaside, wielding a shotgun, shooting pelicans and seagulls. He does chainsaw sculpture. He closes on his 100th real estate sale within 180 days. He rolls on the ground on the 18th hole, after his friend hits an exploding golf ball that he places on a tee. Stuff like that.

He's really a particular type of person, she says.

I think about all of this. He is not doing these things ironically. He is dead serious. Rich and dead. A coffin glazed with gold. And yet it is all performance. He sterilizes any notion of verité.

This is why there needs to be a new kind of acting, I say.

Her mouth purses, like she wants to defend him.

Exhausting, isn't it?

Yes, it is, she says.

What do you have against me? I ask.

You hurt me, she says. I put everything on hold for you.

I didn't ask you to.

You should think about other people when you bring them into your life. If you really want to be with someone, you need to give a shit about what they think, what they do. Everything with you is a one-way street.

True, I say. You're right.

Oliver leans in. I'm working to be empathetic, he says to us. And entertaining.

Like I said, Zozotte says, go find yourself a seat.

Is it over? I ask.

There will always be something between us, she says.

Oliver continues. I'm working to be a deep thinker and a people person—I will now never eat lunch alone again—to actualize my full potential, save money and give my money away, and be outraged by injustice. Be clean, stylish, a pet person, a socially engaged person, politically relevant, a clean eater, not addicted to, for the most part, drugs—apart from M—a vacationer, and also recognized, and OK with being recognized for my accomplishments.

Zozotte has her own warm up strategy. At every item in Oliver's list she carries through with a different reaction.

The show starts in five minutes, she says. She stands there looking at the wall. I tell her goodbye. She will not look back, but she says goodbye with finality.

III.

A proper stage is a palette. Bare and lit, shadowy almost. Empty, it speaks out that it is meant to be filled with the paints of movement, life, action. As I look around the theatre—it is small— one hundred seats—I feel compassion and anger. How passive it all is. My seat is in the front and so I walk there and look back at them—they, the audience—and they are all aglow and prepared for the show of it. I sit. I settle in with a thoughtful hand propping up the side of my head.

Oliver takes the stage. He approves of the silence. He grows from it and builds so that the stumbling questions he asks are shared. And then he lashes out at himself. We all peer into his self-hating soul and long with him rather than against him.

In the next scene, a love for Avril and a love for Zozotte reside. Oliver continues on. The other players play. The Brute, in tight-fitting T-shirt is jilted. Avril is broken by Oliver's zeal. Zozotte's heart rises to the top. She is pure and lovely, and we cannot fathom why she allows herself to be subsumed into Oliver's searching love. He is unworthy of her and yet he triumphs. One by one the Brute, Avril, and Zozotte fall away in their own way until Oliver is left only with his camera. He manipulates it and fetishizes it until it establishes itself as its own character. In it, the image and the ideal reign. The intermediary of the camera is king, not the people it serves, and I am touched by what has taken place.

Somehow, the Impresario has done something special. It all falls into place and I see the wisdom in how the Impresario has battled with Oliver's camera. That Oliver had to fight to keep the camera in the play, means that the camera is the window in for him and for the audience. The Impresario could have snatched it away at the last minute, but he didn't. In not doing it, it meant so much more, ultimately. What a prop can do if it is well-handled!

Everyone here is stricken by the performance. Clearly, something significant has just happened. It is the communal power of the stage that has brought us all together under the Impresario's successful orchestration. I feel the elevated feeling such that I remain sitting in my seat as I do not want to disturb what has settled over all of us in this place.

The Impresario has managed to adequately develop a look, a tension, an environment—many other thoughts to think, everything swelling around everyone, in that the actors break in on each other and build up a message, so that there is much to do and think simultaneously in every scene. Two dimensions, three dimensions, all kinds of heaviness. Instead of single, solitary, isolated interactions, there is a believable suite of ascending gravity. The play is a success.

I am thinking camera camera camera, and I attempt to make sense of this imprint on my mind. No, the camera is not so important, it is only a prop. Instead, it is what we make of it. I have a camera, now what? How will I proceed?

My mind hums. I stay seated long after the audience releases out into LA.

Balance, I say to myself. Pad kid poured curd pulled cod.

As I sit in the theatre seat, Blathner approaches me from behind, breaking my focus from the empty stage. He sits next to me. He smells of Old Spice and wears a musty threadbare sport coat. He is in earnest.

Your brother won't sign the releases, he says.

Why would he? I ask.

Says he doesn't need the money.

Did you insist? By the way, your skin looks good.

Thank you. Do you know how difficult you people are?

Us actors? Us Gargons?

Blathner ignores and continues, I also spoke with Rhony. Rhony's really very motivated by the novelty of it. And he's made a lot of progress on your suit. He says he has a prototype, and we can take it out for the big thing tonight. We're meeting at Lake Hollywood to do a camera test. A crew has been prepping the spot ever since Foster gave this idea the go ahead. We drew up the scene, so now everything can proceed.

There's a problem, I say.

Yeah?

Do you really think we can gain traction in the psychosomatic development of America?

It's a commercial, Blathner says.

Everything is a commercial, I say. The question is, really, what is this commercial a commercial for? I was worried for a while that you had some sort of impetigo on your neck. I believe in the film, so I believe that this commercial is a commercial for something worthwhile. But how can we make it mean something more than just the sum of its parts?

That's your job, Blathner says. My neck is fine.

I nod. Then I respond, I guess the question is, how do we get at Foster's goal?

Unfilmable, Blathner says.

That's what I said.

You were right.

I cannot accept that, I say. You know, what the Producer did, giving me that envelope, it really made me think about why I am doing what I am doing.

Don't worry, you'll get paid.

Will I?

It's the only thing I really know anything about.

Paid for you is different than paid for me, I say.

Let's get going.

Blathner ushers me back and out of the theatre, and we walk to a valet stand set up for the steakhouse a block over. I ask for a cigarette. He says, those'll kill you, and I tell him, as a samurai, I'm already dead. He doesn't laugh. He gives me a Pall Mall. I give it back to him. I just kind of asked for it in order to say it, I say. I take out a Gauloises, light it on the hot end of Blathner's Pall Mall, and work on handling it with fluidity.

His car shows up. It is not the same car I busted out of last night. You have two Sebrings? I ask.

What's it to you? he says.

Nothing, I say. But I'm impressed.

We get into the car, still holding our cigarettes, and we drive.

Picasso said, For me to draw like Raphael was easy, but I had to learn to draw like a child. I consider this as I engage in a variety of stretches and resistance exercises atop the squeaky pleather upholstery in the passenger seat. Philip Glass playing, Blathner wheels recklessly around corners in that way that usually leads to a heavy loss of hubcaps. He comments that the suspension is splashy. I think about how to look closely, and at the same time not just simply see what I want to see.

I think about the poet writing about pain. There are radiating lines issuing outward from every hurt, touching upon every person in concentric circles from its origin. Oliver hurts, the actors suffer, the audience feels. My family hurts, my brother acts out, there is no peace, I am able to perform generously. Zozotte draws inward, I am left in the lurch, nothing satisfies, nothing anyone wants from me is given them. *We all hurt / we all have been hurt. / One window leads to another / we pause to mourn / for one more fallen friend. // Our heads always down / we wait for the great people to tell us. / We once waited for the great people.*

The main thing is to keep the main thing the main thing, says Blathner.

There are exercises that work, I say, and exercises that don't. They are both ways of working things out. There is a distinction between the subject of the painting and the object being painted.

It's all process, he says.

But it is invasive. And all the world really cares about is the processed.

The message must be packaged, Blathner says.

I die bearing witness, I add.

We drive on. I look out the window. I watch all kinds of signage fly by.

The Producer will be at the lake, Blathner says. He'll want to talk to you.

I guess the body is communal, I say.

You should listen to him.

We drive on, and though it is night and well beyond the hours of the workday commute, the freeways are clogged with cars. People are intent on being corralled to wait with seemingly no progress. We are one such group.

Blathner's mood is one of intense readiness. He is as active as he can be, moving his smoldering Pall Malls from hand to hand, and holding the half-empty pack in an opposite hand while driving with his forearms. I have had my third cigarette of the day, and I use the desire to smoke another as a method of attenuating my neck from my body. This activity, and that I am sitting enclosed in Entrefacado Blathner's second best Chrysler Sebring helps me think a long certain fine line. Now that commercial entertainment has dethroned avant-garde work, we've come to a place where avant-garde work has again become relevant, and yet unviable commercially.

What's the plan? I ask Blathner.

Shouldn't we all be asking you? he says. His neck has healed nicely but his face looks like a mayonnaise sandwich left out to bake in the sun. His phone purrs.

I can't believe how old your phone is.

Yep, he says. Speaker.

It's Foster. Hey, you two—look—I just want to say we're really getting some good work done—how do you feel?

I say I feel fine.

Blathner asks, Just how much of the material that we've filmed is useable?

An obscene amount, Foster says. We're really happy over here—it's obscene—almost all of it—at least from a director's perspective—we're actually really very happy over here—but it's the voiceover that really matters from a certain perspective—we've got all these new digital programs to link up the voiceover with the film—I can't wait to get into the sound booth to lay down some audio—really altogether very happy—I can't stress that enough.

This is good news, Blathner says.

It is, says Foster.

Also, Blathner says, we're wondering over here, what's the plan for Lake Hollywood?

Yeah—I hear you, Foster says, it's crucial—I hear you—so at this set up, Godot, you have no audible lines of dialogue—know that.

This is fine, I say.

Fine, so—yeah—what it is, is this scene is a montage of naked male and female bodies—these bodies are not too fat, not too thin, not perfect—they're scattered about face down in the grass, apparently asleep or dead or whatever, motionless—and Insalubre walks around among them—he ducks in and whispers a few words into the ears of a few of the people here and there—the people lying face down—and after he walks among them, they get up and wander off—they get up one at a time and look around as if their lives are irreparably changed and then wander off in different directions—but keep in mind, keep in mind—fronting this single continuous shot is a close of the side of Lucia's face—because this is all taking place in the consciousness of Lucia—as she narrates this montage—she's saying—We found each other amidst the best bodies of our generation—we found each other wanting—but the main thing was that we found each other. That's it—then when that scene's over we do the big stunt with you in the suit for the movie promo—sound good?—I'm hearing good things about the production value of the suit.

And when does the lake scene film? Blathner asks.

Tomorrow morning, Foster says.

Very good, says Blathner.

Got it? Foster says.

Got it, Blathner says. Then Blathner tells Foster that we've arrived, and Foster says he'll arrive at the lake late tonight, and hangs up.

We continue on driving through the hills.

Foster thinks the big thing's tomorrow? I ask.

You think Foster's in charge?

We arrive.

We step out of the car, and outside there is a wardrobe trailer, grip trailer, effects trailer, props trailer, and trucks full of lights. I walk past guys with ponytails and metal band T-shirts talking. I negotiate popup tents and barricades, and some towers with spotlights on the top, and I disrobe and walk into the brush fronting the lake. The brush strikes and staggers my legs. It leaves tracks. I walk up to the edge of the lake and plunge myself into the water. It is not cold. Can I only love someone for an hour? Can I prove that a certain gesture is genuine? Can I ever know someone is pleased to see me? If big black bats could blow bubbles, how big of bubbles would big black bats blow? The ochre ogre ogled the poker. There was a minimum of cinnamon in the aluminum pan.

I swim a bit and hold my breath. I notice there is someone swimming next to me in a neoprene suit. The surface tension of the water parts. It's the PA. It's the same one who's been snipping holes in every prop I've touched.

This time she asks. She asks for a shock of pubic hair. She says she wants to snip it off herself, underwater, in the dark, using an underwater flashlight, with her own gloved hand. That it will not hurt. Why would it?

Why ask permission? I ask.

I've gained a certain respect for you, she says.

So, before you were collecting without respect?

She doesn't answer. It seems easy for her to tread water.

I tell her I am calling her the Artifactor. I tell the Artifactor that I need her help with tonight's publicity stunt.

That's what PAs are for, she says, through her respirator.

I whisper quietly and intensely what I want her to do into the side of her head through her wet diving hood. She agrees, then I give her assent. She disappears under the water, and I tread in the stillest possible way as she quickly and painlessly does what she needs to do, and I barely even feel a tug.

She pops up from her task, her face streaming wet, her face wearing a not altogether satisfied look.

I have a theory about what you mean by this, I say, but I want to proceed through a line of questions that might help shed light on certain events that have unfolded in my life of late.

She is able to tread water quite comfortably due to her diving equipment. I, on the other hand, steadily tread water with much difficulty, but also very productively, workout wise. I can not yet feel the burn, but I am enthusiastic about what the results will be of me beating my legs and waving around water with my hands.

She pops the respirator out of her mouth. Go ahead.

What do you do, I ask, with all these tender bits of my life?

I keep them, she says. I keep them in vials and label them for safe keeping. Her brow is knitted. Her face is dappled with freckles like bark. I guess you could say I collect them.

To what end?

You are an artist, she says. I am an artist, she says. I assume you understand art when you see it?

I do, I say, but is it art qua art, or are you saying something? And if you are, what is it that you are saying?

It's my collecting, she says. That's my statement. I'm always looking out for things to put in jars. When I heard about this film, how it was being shot, I watched you, saw how everything you do is oracular. I decided I needed to get a piece.

I would like to make some observations and perhaps some interpretations, I say. First, I would like to state some facts.

She bobs in the lake with generous control. The moon is up and there is nighttime light everywhere. Nothing is in darkness.

I have noticed you, I say. I noticed you on set and you are pretty facile. But I would like to say, you are working in a way that makes your employment tenuous.

Yes.

One wrong move means you will lose your PA job and you will be banned from set. Does that worry you?

You assume a lot.

Not at all. It's why I ask.

Because there's no danger in me losing my job.

Are you kidding? I ask. One bad move and you are banned. You could even be removed from the set for all you have already done.

Have you tried to get me banned? Do you even know my name?

I have not. I do not. But I know you are the PA with chagrin. The one with the taciturn brow. Black hair. Freckles. Never seems to be where she needs to be when things need to be done. But all that is inconsequential, because in reality you are treating this film like your own personal scavenger hunt.

It's all I can do, she says. You should understand this most because you are an actor. All a character can do all the time is to operate at 100 percent. We don't choose our roles. We can't just turn it off. It surges out of us like a waterfall.

There where love awakens dies the I, dark despot, I say.

Who said that? she asks.

Freud, Rumi, Che Guevarra.

It's perfect, she says.

I respect your work, I say, how you have forgotten all about the I. How all you have is your art. Her neoprene-covered shoulders jostle up and down. So, I am hoping you can shed light on a certain puzzle I have in my life.

Yes?

If you were confronted by an authority figure, someone who is in effect your boss, and that boss were to give you an empty envelope, and a lot of emphasis was put on that envelope, what would you make of it?

You're asking what an empty envelope means?

I am not, I say. I am asking what it means to you. I thought you might have a theory, being that apparently you are a bit of a collector.

I guess, she says, I'd have to say that the envelope means something. But that what was or was supposed to be in the envelope is the more important thing. Money? A letter? Some kind of official document?

People do not read letters anymore, I say.

Then I'd have to say money, or a contract. A check. That's what's important.

Why?

Because you're asking about it. And it seems you care a lot. You can't just accept that the envelope was given to you as is without contents. There must be something more, you ask. There has to be.

You are right, I say. You are.

She slaps the water with her palms to make a splash. I think you're paralyzed by your fear of what's inside other people. And besides, I know a lot about containers. A container is beautiful. It represents possibility.

But it is also a negative space.

That's your view.

This is all so very incisive. Thank you.

You're welcome.

Another question.

Of course.

Are you certain you will help me with the black curtains that I asked you to help me with?

She looks offended. Of course I will. Right now?

Now.

Goodbye, she says. She disappears down in a well of water, and I track what I think is her intended direction, but then she doesn't resurface where I expect her to resurface, and I tread water for a while, scanning around in every direction for her to emerge from the lake. She does not.

My energy begins to run out, so I swim to the shore and emerge on the bank, dripping, with limbs rubbery from the workout.

I walk back to the center of the compound and the staging area in the ready-made trailer park, and I stop in the middle and call out for a PA. A PA shows up and tells me where wardrobe is, but the PA does not know where the super-secret place is where the suit for the big act is being assembled. I tell her to go find out, and she disappears, and I walk to wardrobe to get something on.

In the wardrobe trailer, I struggle to find something exactly perfect. I decide on black bicycling pants and a tight-fitting anorak, black ankle socks, and black running shoes. There are no climbing shoes in the entire trailer. I pull the anorak's hood tight over my ears. It envelops my head in a mass of black. It is time.

The biggest trailer in the compound is important in that it signifies power. It commands the center. It demands protection and control. I walk toward it directly. It has that mannered subtlety that important structures bear in LA. It is stripped of adornment. It is only noticed when looked at in order to be seen.

The guy with the headset standing outside fences the door, and yet he indicates by his ready acknowledgment of my presence that he wants me to enter the trailer right away. In fact, after he exchanges a greeting with me and a greeting over the squawk box that announces inside the trailer what is happening outside the trailer, he gets assent, and he nods, and he opens the door for me, and sends me in.

I enter the place, and there is a very small and tasteful desk crammed in near a wall, and a man, the Producer, is sitting with his back to me, facing quite a large piece of expensive Abstract Expressionist art. He appears to be considering the art, his halo of grey hair resting sweetly atop his head.

You were not my first choice as a replacement for my first choice for this role, he says.

I sit on the edge of a low chair placed in front of him and lean forward, my elbows on my knees.

He continues, I want the film to be recognizable as something significant. I want the film to be funny and rich emotionally, and in a way that makes money. And above all, I want the film to be big in China. The Chinese Ministry of Entertainment is the perfect gauge of whether or not a film is of global consequence. In short, they know entertainment. In spite of, or in fact, maybe even because of the language barrier, this is the case. Say what you will, but they only pick winners. In fact, they ensure that they are.

So then, why did you allow me into the picture? I ask.

Foster says you're significant. Foster says you're funny. Foster says you're rich emotionally. And I agree. I look at you, I look at the rushes. Foster was right. You are doing something everyone will recognize, if not now, eventually, something no one has ever seen before.

And what's that?

The portrayal of happiness.

I guess this is where the funny comes in.

Yes, it's funny. It's spectacle funny. Kitch. But I can't yet tell if it will translate into Yuan. China only allows a handful of films each year. Usually only blockbusters, but what we're trying to do here is to open up a new vein. We get China, we double our reach. They're equal to the U.S. in terms of receipts. We instantly double our money.

That is happiness.

It's a new vein.

But this is more of an art film, I say.

You're a trailblazer. Don't you consider yourself a trailblazer?

I do not know what to say. The Producer is insane. You're insane, I say.

The Producer swivels around so that I can see his face. I don't care what you think. What I want you to do is to promote the hell out of this movie. You have all our resources at your disposal. Go out and do your work.

All I need is the marquee, I say.

You have it.

It is important to learn how to kick guys in the balls, how to hit other people in order to cause maximum pain, how to grab a person by their clothes so they can be easily thrown to the ground. And I have learned to love violence. In the theater of cruelty in which I am engaged, people are actors and actors never stop to question their roles. We ascend together. We ascend through pain. I leave the Producer fully conscious of what I must do next. I step down onto the hard pan parking lot. I look around for another

PA. Everyone is busy prepping the field next to the reservoir for tomorrow morning. I ask around. I see metal bars being carried. Boxes are on rollers. Golf carts are trucking gear. The entire place is lit with overhead cans that shine light directly downward at the ground, I guess to avoid light pollution in the surrounding hills.

I decide to find my trailer. Where it is I do not know, and wearing all black, no one notices me, so I have to grab a guy in a flannel and highwater slacks, wearing a toolbelt, and ask where it is.

He sees me, looks again and kind of balks. Hey, he says. Want me to show you?

No, just tell me.

It's over there next to those yellow Christmas lights.

Cheers, I say.

Hey, he adds. Where can I see more of your work? There's nothing out there.

You mean online?

Anywhere, he says. To see anything, I have to go to the dailies.

Me too.

I leave him wanting, and I walk over toward the trailer and up the steps. I throw open the door and find Rhony. He's wearing teal wristbands and teal running shorts. He's looking at the suit hanging from a metal truss.

You! he says.

I look at the suit. It looks like black gunmetal pleated with whorls, like tactical armor made of black Cool Whip. Like a stealth fighter meant to be worn. I gather the sleeve in my hand. It is luxurious and substantial. I think you nailed it, I say.

Have you ever seen Rodin's sculpture of Balzac? he asks.

I think, I say. *Monument to Balzac*?

That's it, he says. Is it like you dreamed?

It is so.

So, since you've seen it, you'll get it. That's what I'm going for.

Is Rodin your guy?

Oh no, he says. Not at all. But he's yours.

One thing Rodin said, I tell him, he said to Rilke, Teach your-self to see. I think that is what you are getting at.

So you'll wear it?

Of course, but tell me what you think of this shoot.

You don't wanna know what I think, he says. I don't know anything about movies.

But what do you see?

I see infrastructure. I see all my friends with lousy parts. I see doom, darkness, all these points of view stacking up and blocking each other out. But what do I know?

And that is what you have put into this suit?

You got it. Darkness, suffocation, frustration. That's a lot of it.

Is it finished?

Yeah. And I have the backpack right here.

Rhony pulls a big horizontal board up from beside the table and it has huge lightbulbs on it in a strip. It has a thick shimmering golden border. The bulbs spell out the words *TONE POEM*.

And it is ready to be worn? I ask.

This is it, he says. You fasten the harness over your shoulders and flip the switch. The backpack holds the light source as well and the billboard part lights up. Huge wattage. Thousands of candles. Makes you a walking marquee.

It is what Blathner and Foster had in mind—the whole point of the suit.

I strip, except for the anorak, and he holds up the suit so I can get into it and put it on over the top of me. He tightens up the straps at various places and makes it sure. It is sturdy at all points, and he is able to ratchet it into place with hidden pulls and levers here and there along the arms and the legs and around my thighs. He zips it up. He slings the marquee on over my shoulders, and se-cures the lacework of plastic cords and the harness. It is very snug, and I am suited up with the horizontal transom like the beam of a cross of crucifixion.

I flip the switch. I put on black gloves, and I pull the hood over my head.

Rhony looks at my face and takes out a roll of black tape and attaches the edges of the hood around my head to my forehead and my cheeks. He embraces me.

I return the gesture and turn around and have to carefully exit the trailer sideways. Everything behind me is lit up, and it is dark outside, and I begin walking away from the trailer.

I aim myself up the hill, and the smell of the brush and the weeds in the outer reaches of Griffith Park seem out of place. It is heavy and earthy all around and like a nature walk. Everything about it is LA-esque. This reminds me that nothing is meant to grow here in Southern California. That even the brush that covers the hillsides has been imported to control erosion. Erosion the central concern here. May nothing erode the constructions we are meant to live upon.

From where I am I can see the Hollywood sign. No need to light a night light on a light night like tonight. The brush brushes me. Tie twine to three tree twigs. On a lazy laser raiser lies a laser ray eraser.

I proceed, the marquee on my back. The light that shines from it marks my position in the brush as I climb the trail leading up to the major backbone of the ridge. My thighs feel strong and lithe as the marquee tags the bushes that I squeeze in between. It makes every foot I can climb a kind of victory. And it really is. I have gotten past what was keeping me back—that feeling that I was betraying myself by not donning the suit with the marquee. And the suit is so beautiful, and the marquee is so perfectly executed.

I stop to get my bearings. Behind me is a city of lights, their pinpoints oppose the harsh velvet black. Below me is the staging area, and I can see the crew squirreling production fodder from place to place. Some standing around talking on phones. They are all distracted. As I look out at the view, I hear a light buzzing. Among the crickets and the bugs making their own music, the buzzing could seem commonplace, but it is not. It is distinctly different, unnatural, and it grows louder. It captivates me. I attempt to locate it. It appears to be coming from the sky.

Now I can see a few light emitting diodes. They are green and moving in a flurry. The noise is issuing from a camera drone. There it is, a witness to the brutality. I take another moment and scan the production area more carefully, systematically. I see the young guy in the bandana. He's looking up at me, and then the drone, and he has a tablet with a screen attached to the top of his handheld controls. It lights up his face in a flood of brightness. He controls the drone remotely.

I make my way up to the ridge. I move forward, impelled by haste, my motion restrained by the buffeting of each bush on the crossbeam. Quickly, quickly, quickly, three times fast. Quickly, quickly, quickly. A slimy snake slithered down the sandy Sahara. If colored caterpillars could change their colors constantly, could they keep their colored coats colored properly? I thrust my fists against the posts and still insist I see the ghosts. End of day LA stretches far and away down its valleys and hills below and beneath all along on their way to its reaches where the day has ended and the sun has descended, and I move along on my way.

Minutes, then an hour. I come near the great white Hollywood sign on the ridge. But around this there are fences, and I look for evidence that the Artifactor has made it up here before me. The electrified fence has indeed been cut, and I test it for shock with my hand. It does not shock.

I pull in the marquee sideways, and I slip through the opening and around the foot of the enormous, white *D*. I see the piles of black fabric the Artifactor has staged around the base of the letters on the ground. I look up, and a ladder has been leaned against the back of the great letter *D*. I arrange myself so the drone can get a good approach shot. I waste no time. I grab a great portion of the fabric and stretch it out and take a gusset at one end and attach a cable through its reinforced hole. I trust that the drone is still hovering out there, its lenses still on me.

I ascend the ladder, holding the cable, and as I get to the top I glance around back behind the sign. I see the Artifactor far down below on a dirt road on the other side. She has been cuffed up by a cop and is being put into a police SUV. She is being driven away.

When we fail to avert our eyes we are stuck, we are dead, we are artists, we are idolators. We cannot get beyond the consequences of what our gazes have fixed themselves on. From that point on, all we have are pharmaceuticals or crazy. We really cannot handle that infinity.

In an hour of hard work, I drape black drape up over the letters *WOOD*, and I rush to finish. There is a violent hammering in the sky. A police helicopter begins to strafe the hillside with a searchlight. They're calling out warnings by bullhorn, wanting to talk me down. The camera drone is still present and that little thing maintains my confidence. I climb up and pull the drape atop one of the *L*s as the authorities close in. I finish. *HOL Y*. Two heavily-geared cops rappel from the copter and bang into me. They knock my arms together, zip tie my hands, and attach me to two of their ropes. I give in easily without a struggle. They smirk at each other. Don't do anything brave, one of them says. They tear the words *TONE POEM* off my back and drop them to the ground below. I do not fight.

On the ground, I am hustled into a cop car. As the door shuts, an envelope flies in through the side of the ajar door and lands in my lap. I look to see who threw it through the window, but do not see anything. My hands are cuffed so I cannot get at it. It is just sitting there in my lap, and I am looking at it. A cop sees me doing what I am doing and opens the door and grabs the envelope.

What's this? He asks. He tosses it onto the ground. Junk mail, he says. Ha ha.

Open it and read it, pretty please, I demand.

Where did it come from? he asks.

The window, I say.

He shakes his head and leans down to pick it up. He looks at it, and says it's to Godot, from B.F.

Ask nicely, he says.

Be your best friend?

He pauses. He has basic acting chops. He tears it open and takes out a piece of paper folded over—a half of a sheet.

How can I forgive you? the cop reads. *You told the secret story of our family to the world. You have no shame.* How melodramatic, the cop says. He reaches in the window to where I am sitting and places the open sheet on my lap.

It is not true. I am all about shame. Instead of looking at the note and reading it, I make myself conscious of the meaningful posing that all good artists employ in their work. Everything. A covered eye, the hue of a face, a shock of long hair. Size and proportion in relation to the audience. All of this works together to synthesize into something that says what we need to say. It is not only the method of meaning, but the meaning which matters, and the meaning tied up in the great union between all people. True love of self, true love of neighbor, and a union with what is divine is its aim.

Here, the conclusion of my memory. And because of my search, pursued by the authorities, I trespassed. Under that sign, and in that way, I have arrived at a way to finally ask forgiveness. I will go to my brother and ask him. But whether I am forgiven or not, it matters not. Just in confessing that it is me, not him, I have finally found something holy. True, I am guilty, but I am also not beyond making amends. I will soon be traveling too fast in a car through the streets of Los Angeles. But for now, here, I can rest, I can collapse into a peaceful sleep and think about how everything might have been different, and how I did my best so that what was filmed was just so.

Acknowledgments

Sincere thanks to Ryan Griffith, Scott Lucy, Stephen-Paul Martin, Adam Pike, and Kara Seto Silke for help in shaping these sentences through advice and encouragement.

I am also indebted to my parents Gerald and Karen for their tireless love and support.

Thank you to Sandra Alcosser, R. Anthony Askew, Stephan Cook, Paul Delaney, Matt de la Peña, Katie Farris, Janet Fitch, John Fox, Judith Freeman, Mary Garcia, Ryan Griffith, Emily Hicks, Harold Jaffe, Chuck Laham, Gerald Locklin, Shelly Lowenkopf, Meagan Marshall, Stephen-Paul Martin, Bill McCurine, Ryan J. Jack McDermott, Steve Montgomery, Stephanie Mood, Mark Moore, Brighde Mullins, Jessica Pressman, Judy Reeves, Aram Saroyan, Bassam Shamma, Karl Sherlock, and Rita Williams for personal instruction in the art of writing.

And endless gratitude to the team at Wipf and Stock for making this book a reality.

S.D.G.

Made in the USA
Las Vegas, NV
07 November 2021

33939354R00063